In order to move forward, one must first accept what was, what is and, what could be."

-author unknown

This book is a work of fiction. Names, characters, businesses, organizations, places, events and incidents either are the product of the author's imagination or are used fictitiously. Any resemblance to actual persons, living or dead, events, or locales is entirely coincidental.

For information contact :Christina08021@hotmail.com

Book layout and design by Christina Collins

Back Photo by Syd Redmond Photography

ISBN-13 978-0692126035

Saving Chelsea

By: Christina Collins

Acknowledgments

To My Creator

No greater love is there than your love ...Thank you for your mercy, grace and kindness, without you I would be nothing! It is threw you I have learned the true definition of love. I will forever be indebted to you...Thank you !

"Zion"

Son, as a little girl I would lay awake at night and dream to one day have a voice and be heard by people all over the world ...I wanted people to hear me, feel my poems, read my stories and be inspired. In my heart I believed it would happen and I never lost sight of my dream regardless of where life took me, I always knew writing was a part of my journey. I see the same fire in you. You have dreams and passions, even at a young age and I admire that about you! Whatever those dreams may be hold on to them, God gave you this for a reason. They will keep you awake at night, they will unsettle you, they will make you cry and make you smile at times. They will be your place of peace and fuel at the same time but, never forget them; they serve a purpose to help shape your legacy that will affect the world.

My prayer is that when you pick up this book, feel its pages and read its words that it is a constant reminder that with God's love, your hard work and drive that those dreams are possible! Remember, always use your mind, feel with your heart, and never lose sight of your dreams. Anything is possible when you work hard and believe. The world is your oyster…

Mother

Mom…The gateway in which I've came through this plane of existence…Always remember how beautiful you are and never ever stop smiling, Never stop dancing and most importantly, never stop loving! And one last thing..It is okay to choose YOU sometimes..You've worked hard.. It is your right! Thank you for all you've done for me ...I Love you!

Daddy

Daddy, Thank you for choosing me as your daughter and for that I will always love you. It wasn't easy I'm sure but, you have to admit there was never a dull moment. Thank you for all the fatherly advice you've given over the years and now as a woman.. I can appreciate it!

To My Brothers and Sisters

Sean, Jay, Jackie, Carmella, Sierra, and Raymond…I couldn't have picked a better bunch to have as siblings in this life. All of the support, love, and crazy memories have been so important in my life. Thank you for always accepting me for who I am even when it may have been hard for you to see me in the moment your love for me made you understand. No matter how far apart we may be; whether New Jersey, Seattle, or Philadelphia, we will always be together in my heart. Please know, no one else could have contributed to this body of work unanimously the way you guys have. Our experiences have given me plenty of writing material over the years (Smile) if I had the opportunity to do it all over again and choose, it would always be each and every one of you!

The Loved, the Unforgotten

Aunt Marcia, Auntie… Oh how I miss your spirit, your courageous demeanor, and your smile. Thank you for always encouraging me to write. You were one of the first to even care about my work and for that I will always be grateful. I can still hear your voice telling me to be beautiful in all things, on paper, inside, and in the mirror. I hope wherever you are you are proud of me. I love you!

Adebayo, how could I publish my first book without saying thank you? The way you saw this world and your vast knowledge always challenged me to expand my mind outside of the tiny world I was in. I remember when I was so big-headed about my first book and I came to you to be the first to review it. It took you all but one day to hand it back to me, Look me in the eyes and say : "That's great but, you can do better.. I know you!" I was crushed yes, but, in my heart of hearts I knew you were right and it fueled me to start over, truly challenge myself and this book was the end result. I hope wherever you may be your smiling in comfort that I finally got it right. Our 17 years of friendship will never be forgotten …you always kept it real with me and for this I will always be grateful! Thank you!

LOV3

Thank you for the lessons of patience, joy, and compassion. Words can't express the appreciation I have for you. In my heart you will dwell forever.

" Love is patient, love is kind. It does not envy, it does not boast, it is not proud..."

-I Corinthians 13:4
New International Version (NIV)

Table of Contents

Introduction

DAMN IT !...I BROKE MY LIPSTICK!! NOW MY MAKEUP is going to look a mess! It's bad enough I put way too much eyeliner under my left lid and now it looks like I stepped into a boxing ring. This always happens when I'm rushing out the door in the morning, carrying several bags on one arm, holding a cup of coffee in one hand, a broken lipstick in the other, along with a horrible attempt to apply it. I mind as well balance a giant ball on my head and add to the circus.

Lately, my life has been a Barnum and Bailey production with me as the ring leader. Sometimes it seems I just can't get right ever since the day Morgan left two years ago. But, every morning I wake up and put my best foot forward with a smile in an effort to get this life of mine together. "The universe unfolds as it should in all things great and small...everything happens for a reason." A wise person once told me as I watched Morgan, my close friend strapped to a gurney and hauled away to a mental facility two years ago. She had a mental breakdown, called the cops and tried to take her own life after politely throwing her expensive art and furniture from a third story window in the middle of Rittenhouse Square while laughing hysterically. She lost everything. Her job, most close friends and still remains there to this day. It affected me more than I realized at the time. Funny how someone else's crazy can drive you right into a crazy space with them.

How could this woman, who in my eyes had it all; just lose it. She was beautiful, intelligent, successful, a bit erratic at times but for the most part pulled together. Morgan had it all figured out or, at least I thought so. She did have her moments of being withdrawn and refrain from the world but hell; the average person does that after a hard day's work. This could have happened to anyone. Her situation shed light on a void inside of me that I always knew was there. Like the dirty laundry, you continue to step over and keep putting off till one day the smell almost knocks the wind out of you then you have no choice but to make time to fix the funky dilemma.

I knew something had to give or the stinky void within me would only get worse. This unfulfilled feeling was hovering over me so; I started looking for the answers in an effort to not end up the same way Morgan did, Out of control, sad, and trapped in her own head.

This new found determination led me in every direction. I tried everything from meditating and chanting to long Sundays in a church. I began to take a serious look into Islam at a local library until I smelled the new Baconator sandwich at the Wendy's next door and realized I could never give up any succulent piece of bacon. I even considered Judaism at one point till I realized they would never have me. My co-worker suggested a great way to shake this funk was to start opening up, pay attention, wake up, listen to the things around me and embrace life in its entirety.

Maybe the universe had something it was trying to tell me other than "Okay, this is the year you need to lose those 10 pounds you always wanted to shake." The old man's words keep ringing in my head, haunting me, "everything in the universe happens exactly the way its supposed to happen." I decided to document every experience and every person I encounter who contributed along my journey, be receptive and write about it. I didn't want to leave any stone unturned. I know that sounds a bit over the top for the average person, but allow me to introduce myself and then you'll have that *"OOhhhh...Okay, that explains it"* moment.

My name is Alicia D'Amato, a pudgy summer baby from Philadelphia, who enjoys an occasional latte, considered curvy because I'm not a size 6 and has been writing since I could hold a pencil in my hand at the tender age of two. I'm 28 years young, have a roommate named Morpheus who never pays rent but, sheds like crazy, and strolls around the house on four legs like he owns the place, and continuously keeps a resting bitch face. I'm optimistic and cheerful but, can be my own worst critic at times.

Don't worry, I won't bore you to death by providing my autobiography, or spewing out my childhood in a rant because we all have childhood issues and no one wants to hear that but, what I will do is tell the truth, the whole truth, and nothing but the truth...So help me God! There! I am sworn under oath and ready to learn and inspire. So here goes.

The Real Picture

YESTERDAY I AGREED TO A PICTURE WHILE sitting in Center City. The background was slightly distorted, the main angle was a little twisted and the quality overall wasn't the greatest. I had on my glasses accompanied by a huge zit on my right cheek thanks to PMS, and I just so happen to be wearing my old run down timberland construction boots with a pair of tights that didn't make my legs look too hot. My facial expression was perplexed because of the attack of the pigeons who wanted to state their claim to my apple fritter while I sat in their territory. Not to mention the couple who sat across from me who decided to play, "Who can eat who's face faster?" which was interesting at first till I glanced at the vacant spot next to me on the bench that so happened to be occupied by pigeon poop and old water stains. There was so much going on around me that I was certain no one would notice little old me sitting on the bench holding on to a cup of Starbucks for dear life. So, why'd I take the picture in the first place you ask? Aside from the tall photographer with the great smile who offered the free picture, I sat for a quick second and thought..."Why not?" After the old camera spit out the picture I let it dry and quickly glanced at it and of course, I noticed every flaw about me. I began sucking in my stomach and straightening my glasses on my nose all while correcting my posture and then...it began to rain.

I ran into an old coffee house on Samson Street not too far from the bench, sat down and ordered another low-fat latte. As I looked out the window I thought how beautiful the day started out and how the rain had ruined my plans to write outside at the bench. Then I looked down at my semi-wet Polaroid and I couldn't help but smile. As I looked closer in the picture there was a beam of light that shined right over me. What are the odds of that, I thought, for me to take a random picture looking horrible and yet nature was able to make me look radiant and important in the midst of the madness going on in the background, along with my twisted glasses and my disheveled hair?

Suddenly, all the other positive things jumped out of the picture at me and I didn't see all the flaws so much anymore. The tights I had on made me look slimmer, the perplexed look on my face was explained because the couple eating each other's face was somewhat in the picture and the huge zit on my cheek began to look like a beauty mark reminiscent of Elizabeth Taylor's. Ok, maybe I'm reaching with that one but, you get my point. I began to see another side of the picture. The real picture that even on my worst day I should always appreciate the beauty in the flaws...the next time I'm out and about in the city to write...I won't wear a stitch of make-up...I'll just wear me!!

The Shake Down

AS MORPHEUS AND I WERE RELAXING on the couch catching up on what I missed of the Olympics in Rio, while at work earlier, there was a loud knock at the door. Instantly the stress in my upper neck came back. Whenever I get a knock at my door in the evening it's never good. It's either an invite somewhere that I probably shouldn't go because I'll either a) Spend money or b) End up dedicating myself to something that takes me completely out of the way of relaxing "Great! As soon as I crack open a fresh pint of rum raisin ice cream and get comfortable after a long hard day in the office, someone wants something with my life," I thought.

"I am not getting off this couch," I told Morpheus and he made the "Yeah right" face, yawned, turned his attention back to the Olympics and disregarded me as usual which tends to happen often unless I'm opening a can of cat food.

"Boom, Boom" they continued to knock. I decided to quickly grab the remote and turn the T.V. down so whoever was on the outside of the door couldn't hear the cheers from the crowds in Rio during the women's diving competition. Lastly, just in case they had x-ray eyes and could see through the door, I inched further down into the couch and smiled like the Grinch in certainty they would disappear. But, to my surprise, the knocks became more and more intense. "Fine…Fine!" I yelled as I scrambled to put on my bedroom slippers and favorite "leave me alone" fuzzy robe.

"Hold on," I yelled. "I'm coming, I'm coming."

As I looked through the peephole, I couldn't see anything. Then the knock came again and I noticed it was a low knock. I immediately opened the door and it was Ameenah, the cute 8-year-old Spanish girl who lived a few floors up and sold Girl Scout cookies. She was quite the saleswoman and quick on her feet. I promised her 6 months ago I'd always buy her cookies as long as she stayed on the honor roll and did well in school. Well, I had no idea the girl was a mini genius. I've gained 6 pounds and counting since making that promise and she's always on time like clockwork, ready to shove calories and fat -buttery goodness, smothered in chocolate in my face. She's even chased me down in public because I missed my bi-weekly order. Damn me for caring about the education and future of the children. Damn me!

Then, out of nowhere it came to me, if I didn't have cash she'd come back another time and I could easily dodge her until she was sold out. So I grabbed my credit card to play it off and opened the door.

"Hi, Ms. Alicia. I have your usual, and I got a special order in yesterday that I saved just for you. I know how much you like to buy at least four boxes of the chocolaty ones."

Then she pulled something out of her pocket "will you be using cash or credit as she held out her mother's phone with a swipe attachment to process payments. The look on my face I'm sure was priceless.

"Hey, it's kind of late Ameenah, you sure you don't want to come back tomorrow, it's dark out and I'm sure your mommy doesn't want you out this late. I wouldn't want to be the reason you get in trouble, honey. Why don't you run along and catch me another time okay Hunney? Try me again next week." I said sweetly as I began to slowly close the door.

She put her foot in the doorway to stop it from closing. "Nope it's fine as long as I'm in the building," she said while smiling and batting her eyes.

"Will you be having your usual?" she began to add up my order.

I had no idea what I was up against, this little girl was an expert cookie-pusher.

"Fine!" I blurted out. "Give me the usual, and throw in the lemonades. They go down smooth!" I said in disgust that I'd lost a power struggle to an eight-year-old.

"How long have you been doing this anyway?" I asked to be snide.

"Since six…and I've never missed my quota. Okay, that will be $32.50."

"$32.50! You must have miscalculated. I bought six boxes it should only be thirty dollars."

"Yes, but there is a two dollar and fifty cents traveling charge," she said.

"Traveling charge?! You've never added a traveling charge before and as a matter of fact, There is no traveling charge to selling Girl Scout cookies. They are always sold hand to hand so there's no need to add a charge for a quote on quote traveling charge. I used to be a girl scout. I know how this goes, and I know when I'm being HAD! I know what you're doing and it's not gonna work."

"Fine, I'll just cry in the hallway. See what your neighbors will think of you after they hear you cheated a poor girl scout out of two dollars and fifty cents and made her cry."

"You wouldn't," I said.

"Try me!" Said the little spawn of Satan as she leaned over, squint her eyes, and foamed at the mouth.

"This is ridiculous. Where is your mother? I asked her.

"Ahhhhhhhhhh," she screamed in the hallway quickly then stopped.

"Hand over the $32.50 and there'll be no issues. You can get your cookies and I'll be on my way."

"What is this, a shakedown? I asked

Then she began crying louder, so loud Mr. Rodriguez from next door came out into the hallway.

"AHHHHH AHHHHH," she kept crying louder and louder while pointing at me.

"STOP IT right now! Your quite the little saleswoman aren't cha?"

"Here…take it…and it's credit, not debt! Make it fast, and I need a receipt, ya little Pan Handler…oh, and I am no longer a customer!"

"You made a promise and we have a deal!" yelled Ameenah.

"No ! You breached our contract when you decided to add miscellaneous fees. It's called choice service meaning: I have the choice as a customer whether to acquire your services…and I'm choosing not to anymore because you are taking advantage. I initially wanted to help you because I thought you were a little kid trying to raise money for a good cause and I was hoping it would also encourage you to do well in school but, adding extra fees to the prices so you can skim extra money off the top to put in your own pocket is very dishonest. Now, please may I have my cookies? We no longer have business with one another"

"It's called inflation. You have no problem when Whole foods does it," she said.

She then handed over my boxes of cookies, rolled her eyes, and started walking down the hall, then stopped and said, "That's okay…Mr. Jay downstairs in A2 has been asking for the whole shipment of thin mints for the past two months, and I've been reserving them for you. I'm sure he won't mind the price."

Two days later while walking home from Morpheus's bi-monthly trim at Petco I saw Angelo a well-mannered, pretty intelligent 14-year-old who just so happen to be Ameenah's older brother in front of our building washing a brand new car.

The victim in me wondered if I contributed to the down payment.

"Hey Angelo, congratulations on the new family car, its nice" I said

"Oh no, this isn't our car...I wish it was though. I'm just washing cars to get some extra cash."

"That's an awesome way to earn money. Good for you Angelo."

"Yeah, after my dad left, I and my sisters have been doing what we can to bring in the extra cash to help towards my mom's medical bills ever since the cancer spread. It's hard at times, but we do what we can. It may not seem like much but it's five of us so between me, Zion, Saavan and Ameenah we bring in quite a bit."

"Oh, I'm so sorry to hear that. I had no idea your mother was diagnosed with cancer nor did I know Mr. Lopez no longer lived here...I'm so sorry" I told him.

"It's okay, we see him some weekends when he's not working. Are you looking for Ameenah? She's helping out with my mom. She likes to watch the nurses take care of her so she can learn to do it herself. She should be done in about 15 minutes, and then she'll start her cookie rounds. I can tell her you're looking for her."

"Oh, no that's okay. Just do me a favor. I owe her some money. Can you give this to her for me? Thanks?" I asked as I handed over a twenty dollar bill. My guilt made me feel horrible for what I did earlier. Granted she could have been honest and just told me she was hustling to help pay towards her mother's medical bills and I would have definitely helped but it seems someone has much more pride for an 8-year-old than expected. I felt horrible. I knew I had to do something to help out other than a donation of twenty dollars which would yield a nice return of cookies. Sometimes it takes a community to step in and lend a hand. I'd hate to see the children scrambling for money when they are incredibly smart and can use their brain instead of panhandling and hard labor, especially in the technological world we live in.

So I went upstairs to Mrs. Lopez apartment, sat down with Ameenah and Mrs. Lopez. I wanted to show Ameenah how to work smarter, not harder so we started a Gofundme account in which she and Angelo learned to maintain.

Mrs. Lopez also wanted to inspire others so we created a blog tracking her daily progress with her fight with cancer. Within two months we got several hefty charitable donations, loving visits, and warm wishes from people in the community. We even got Mrs. Lopez her own hashtag, #Ms.LopezWins which; spiraled into a mini social media craze and doubled the number of donations.

In six months' time, Ameenah's cookie prices went back down to $5 dollars a box.

Trust Yourself or Trust Someone Else

Every year around Christmas I always do my usual community service. It's my way of giving back since I've been privileged to the things I have. I Help hand out food at a local church on South Broad Street, buy quite a few toys for "toys for tots" and, donate 250 dollars to the Salvation Army. It's the least I can do for the less fortunate. But, last year I broke that tradition. Not that I wanted to voluntarily but, the universe had a different community service in mind …and her name is Casey! Now, before you judge and say I shouldn't call someone community service, hear me out first and I'm sure by the time I am done you'll agree with me far more than disagree. Casey was an old middle school friend who I met in the girl's bathroom during 2nd period. She sang so well it made me believe I could hold a note or two and since that moment we began singing at school in the cafeteria together. I would write her material and sing backup for her, she was the reason I began sharing my writing abilities and stepped out of my shell. After middle school Casey managed to dip in and out of my life. Her family situation at home was never stable because her parents split up all the time. The poor child moved to more states during high school then I've been to in my entire life. I think that may have contributed to her free-spirited nature. She never stayed in one place too long, was highly creative and believed in complete promiscuity in and outside of the bedroom along with being panamorous, it was just a recipe for disaster in her "journey to love", as she calls it. She couldn't commit to something if she wanted to for too long but, always managed to keep in touch and hooked up with me every once in a while to hang out. In high school when she'd move away I'd always receive a random letter or phone call from her updating me on the new ills in her life. She never commanded the attention of the boys in school on purpose but, always managed to attract them with her beauty and free spirit. She had the biggest bushy hair you'd ever seen, a wide smile with perfect teeth and acquired quite a few tattoos on her slender frame as an adult. Casey ate like a horse yet never gained a pound, and dared anyone to say anything about it. She had quite a few talents and led her life by how she felt, if she wasn't passionate about it, there was no way she'd do it. She'd ventured into all kids of   creative professions , after high school she starting designing clothing for women, was a painter for a few months, which surprisingly she sold for a decent amount of money, Then she went to some film school for a year and began filming a documentary on the objectification of women in modern media. The last time we spoke a few years prior she was freelance modeling for a few afro-punk tattoo magazines in New York and loved the couch-hopping life which shouldn't have surprised me when she showed up at my door 6 days before Christmas last year.

I was knee deep in oven cleaner since the day prior I volunteered to bake over 150 cookies for a battered women's shelter in Germantown for the children living there who sought refuge from their mothers abusive partners . Quite a few cookies lost their way and managed to make a mess of my oven. Okay, truth is I had a little too much wine while preparing them and might have sloppily placed a few on the edge of the tray while getting into "Formation" with Beyonce. As I scrubbed up my poor decision from the night before, I heard the doorbell. Annoyed, I rolled my eyes low-key hoping they had the wrong apartment because I didn't want any company. My hair was a mess, my clothes were covered in oven grime and I was partially hung over from the night before.   Then

It rang again so I got off of my sore knees and peeked through the peep hole which was covered by a finger.

"Who is it" I said

"Room service" someone said in a disguised female voice.

"Move it or I'll open the door and let my pit bull out and he hasn't been fed in 2 days" I said as I grabbed and activated my "Pit bull in a can" which I always stashed behind the mosaic vase on my bookshelf by the door. My uncle Sean gave it to me for my 25th birthday and it was a great gift until he stated "I'll never get a man".

Then the person at the door

"Oh please! You've been allergic to dogs since the sixth grade. And, Is that a "Dog in a can?" You can't be serious; I told you just take some self-defense classes. Open up it's me Casey! She said chuckling.

"Oh my God!" I said as I tucked the dog in a can back in its secret spot and quickly opened the door. She immediately hugged me as soon as it came open.

"It's been years, you look great...how have you been? I asked her excited and ecstatic that she was in my doorway and not on the phone.

Why didn't you call me, my number is still the same ya know"

"Well, I wanted it to be a surprise. I'm going to be in Philly for the next couple of weeks doing a few shoots here and there and figured we'd catch up in between. "

As she closed the door behind her I noticed her suitcase and a huge portfolio carrying canvases over her shoulder which led me to believe I was the first person she'd seen since leaving New York.

"When did you get in?" I asked her

"About an hour and a half ago" she said

"Am I the first person you've caught up with?"

First... You're the only. You know I'm funny about the energy I surround myself with, gotta make sure my chi stays on point, ya know?" Second.. My family isn't in Philadelphia anymore remember, I think I may have a cousin or two but, we aren't close. If there's anyone I'd come see in Philly, it's you!" she said as she put her bags in my closet.

Awwwe, Thanks Casey...That's sweet." I said as I put on my kitchen gloves to get back to the filthy oven I was cleaning prior.

"Umm..What are you doing? No, No ..get dressed, I'm treating you to brunch and I'm not taking "No" for an answer. I goggled this vegan spot in Olde City, Apparently they have an awesome chickpea avocado salad. One of the photographers raved about it a few months ago when I was in D.C at a shoot " she said as she strolled through her phone.

"What are you vegan now? …Please, the last time you were here you scarfed down the steak at Delfrisco's so quick the waiter thought he'd forgotten it and brought you another" I said jokingly

"Well, yea..for the moment, you know how I do" she said carelessly as she plopped on the couch.

This didn't surprise me. It was soooo Casey she was always onto a new thing, bored quickly, never consistent and; anyone who opposed her spontaneous lifestyle was quickly eliminated which also didn't surprise me that she didn't have many people here in the city to see. You've gotta love her though, there's never a dull moment.

"As enticing as free food sounds, I really can't right now Casey. I've got to get this oven cleaned, my apartment is a mess, I AM A MESS.. I said as I tapped my lop-sided poorly arranged ponytail

"… and to be honest with you, I'm still kinda drunk from last night… I wasn't planning on going anywhere."

Then she cut me off quickly

"The rules were "You can't say no"

"I didn't say no…I said "I can't right now And besides shouldn't you be checking in soon..it's close to noon..

Where are you staying anyway?" I said hoping to deflect from the peer pressure with my head in the oven.

Surprisingly, there was an awkward silence

"Casey?...I asked her as I removed my head from the oven

"Casey?"

"Yea"

"Are you staying somewhere in the city or are you doing that Air BNB thing near Conshohocken again?

"Hopefully here in the city" She said with her shoulders shrugged and unsure

"Hopefully?!" I said confused

"Well, I wasn't able to find a spot quick enough. A curator at this gallery in Olde City reached out to me last week and needed to meet tomorrow before he heads out of the country for 6 months. It was either now or nothing. He wants to purchase my pieces for his own collection. I'm selling them for 1200 bucks apiece."

Then she went into my closet and grabbed her canvases.

"That's good money and possibly more to come. He's got many friends in the industry. And the only person I know here is you.

"Not true, but okay and I thought you were here to do a few shoots" I said as I rolled my eyes and sighed.

"Well, I booked those immediately after…go big or go home right?" She said.

"Oh god…I think I know where this is going… There's something called a phone, Casey. Why didn't you just call and ask me instead of popping up at my door? For all you know, I could have been out of the country on some exotic island, …or..I don't know… I could have been in here with my man stretched out butt-naked for the weekend. Then you would have really been screwed "

"Really??...Seriously?" she said as she looked at me with her arms crossed in disbelief

" You have NO MAN and the closest you've ever been to going out of the country was probably last week when Calgon took you away" She said

It's not that I don't have a man, I'm on a cleanse to get my mind and body right…Insults will get you nowhere and… That's not the point"

Clearly, I knew she had a point but, the nerve of her to pop up on someone for a week and dish out insults.

"Okay, Okay… I'm sorry for just popping up but, I really need this right now and it would only be for a week. I'll be out of here before the new year."

"Alright…I'm not gonna leave you stranded"

Immediately, she ran over and hugged me

"Thank you, thank you, thank you…Oh my gosh, you are such a lifesaver! It's gonna be like old times. We'll stay up writing and singing all night long, bake those special brownies you use to make, I can even paint you if we hit BLICK tomorrow.. This will be epic. Or maybe we can invite a few hotties over have a party or two, meet some new people…oh god, I've been looking for new energy in my sphere" Casey said hopeful

Usually when Casey talked about "new people in her sphere" that meant she was on the prowl for some new sexual encounters.

Whoa, Whoa… slow down…I have things to do Casey. I had plans before you popped up here .Later today I have to deliver all of these cookies to the shelter, I have to pop into the office to finish up some work and as far as the partying goes..Yes! I am definitely down for that… I have a small Christmas party planned in a few days. Just a few people but, there will be no "Special brownies..Some of these people are my co-workers and I don't want to be the talk of the office because there were "Special brownies". Plus, I haven't done that since college and I don't plan on it!"

Just a few days later before Christmas I went on a cleaning frenzy, trying to get things ready for my annual holiday party. I ended up adding an additional hour to it because Casey was super messy around the apartment. She'd leave hair and old toothpaste all over the bathroom, continuously left dishes in the sink, and turned my living room into a makeshift art studio. I had no idea when I said yes to her staying here she'd be such a slob. I ran out of oilsoap to clean my hard wood floors so I ran to the closest hardware store which ended up turning into a few hours due to Marshalls having a crazy sale. On my way home from Marshalls I called the caterer and made sure they were in route to my house. "Great" I thought, just in time for the party. While in the elevator of my building I smelled a strong weed smell and thought to myself that my neighbor Oma is at it again and should really be a little more considerate, especially since the walls in this building are paper thin and this is a no-smoking building. As I approached my apartment I started thinking of excuses I could give my guests in hopes they would excuse my inconsiderate neighbor. As I opened the door to my apartment, there was Casey, in nothing but her bra and underwear smoking joint and blowing clouds in the air. There were snack wrappers all over the floor, and my favorite bottle of wine I saved for the party was empty.

"Casey!!... What the Hell!!"

"Hey gurl... You want some? She asked with the joint barely in her hand

Noticing the perplexed look on my face she said "Oh, I'm sorry I was just trying to get ready for the parttaaayyy" she said with a high smile. She was so high she stumbled as she tried to stand up.

Infuriated, I dropped my bags and walked straight into my bedroom, closed the door, screamed, and thought of several places I could hide the body after I killed her for inconsiderate stupidity. After fifteen minutes I heard ruffling and mumbling near the door.

"Hey... I take it your mad at me and decided to barricade yourself in there so, I cleaned up the living room, cracked the windows and sprayed some febreze. You can't even tell...I'm sorry" said Casey with her lips pressed closely to the crack of my closed bedroom door.

Too emotionally exhausted from my recent anger and much needed de-escalation I didn't respond and decided to change for the party.

Shortly after getting myself together my company started to show up, the caterer was on time, and I could barely smell the presence of weed because I kept the window open. It was quite chilly but hey, I'd rather explain the chill in the room rather than "My friend, whom is not here, showed up a few days ago and decided to smoke weed in my living room a half hour before you guys came, but don't worry you can't catch contact and your clothes wont smell like it when you leave."

Everything seemed to be going so perfect. Casey stepped out prior to the start of the party. I guess she got the hint and decided it was smart to give me some space. I almost forgot about it until Marcy in the marketing department from my job asked if someone in my building was smoking in the hall. I just brushed it off and blamed it on my neighbor as I originally planned. The party lasted for a few hours and went well. There were plenty of drinks, laughs and smiles. Everyone enjoyed the holiday games, the food and even the DJ didn't miss a beat.

Once the party was over I cleaned up, locked the door and decided to head to bed. I was horribly exhausted from hosting all night long and longed to sleep in. Around 1am before getting in the shower I received a text from Casey saying she was hanging out tonight with some people she met earlier and wouldn't be in. I began feeling a little remorse and did some self-reflecting. While in the shower, I thought about Casey and how I may be a bit hard on her in general; Potentially judgmental on her actions, ideals, lifestyle and decided to have a heart to heart with her in the morning to patch things up besides, we have been   friends for over 10 years and I wasn't willing to lose the bond we once had over a misunderstanding.

A few hours later I was awakened by the toilet flushing. I immediately jumped up with my heart pounding. With the text I received from Casey earlier on my mind, I knew It couldn't have been her so I shook off initial fear and said to myself "Okay Alicia, this is what we've been training for "Break-In /Whoop-ass" mode. I got up, grabbed the pepper spray gel out of my night stand, picked up the phone, dialed 911 and grabbed Leroy from under my bed. Leroy was a wooden bat I'd had since my 2nd year of living alone. I named it Leroy after a freak-ishly large scary friend of my dads who had a reputation for beating up multiple local bullies at the same time when they were kids with nothing but a baseball bat. It was the scariest person I could think of channeling in the event of an attack or break in. I slowly opened the door and peeked out into my hallway, noticed they were still in the bathroom. Then suddenly the door opened up and instantly I swung away so hard I would have definitely hit a home run. It was quite impressive in the moment; I think my father and Leroy would have been proud.

"Oh My God!!" yelled a half dressed woman who fell back into the bathroom.

Surprised, I dropped the bat and proceeded with the pepper spray into the bathroom.

"Who the hell are you and why are you in my apartment?" I yelled

"Please, please don't hurt me ..I just needed to use the bathroom" said the scared woman while holding her head and crying.

"You broke into my house half-dressed to use the bathroom?" I said puzzled and pissed off.

"No, Casey told me when we got here I could get some Advil out the medicine cabinet if I needed, please..Don't hurt me.. I just needed Advil!"

What?" I said completely confused

I then grabbed the bat in anticipation of more surprises, walked into the living room turned on the light only to find Casey buried under several covers on my sofa bed.

Casey!...What the hell is going on?" I yelled

"Huh?" said Casey as she climbed from under the covers

"Why are you yelling? What's going on? She asked

confused and drunk.

Then the covers started moving and I got in swing mode again. I anticipated giving Leroy another go out of frustration and fear. Another head popped up from under the covers.

"Who turned the lights on?… Oh hey Alicia" said Jay, the ladies' man of the block from the apartment building across the street. Jay was an art dealer who was infamous for partying hard, kept a wide array of woman on his arm, and was quite a savvy dresser.

"Casey, get up! Why do you have random people in my apartment without asking me? What is wrong with you?" I yelled

"What is wrong with me? She said as she stood up

"What's wrong with you? You're yelling at me like I'm a child and in front of my company… God Alicia it's like 4 am!"

Yes, it is 4 am Casey". I said enraged.

"Ever since I got here you've been doing nothing but, yelling at me and complaining like you're my mother…It's ridiculous" said Casey

"…Do you realized I almost killed a stranger whom you allowed in my house without asking or telling me, And to add insult to injury you have THE NERVE to act as if I'm wrong for being upset. You said you weren't even going to be here tonight. I locked the door …how did you even get in here"

"I had a key made" she said casually

Then Jay said "Can everyone just please stop yelling, it's 4 am"

"Get out Jay!" I yelled louder

"Is that quiet enough for you.. Get out of my house!" I said as I grabbed his pants off the floor and threw them at him

"As a matter of fact …Everyone out Now!"

"Alicia what are you doing?" Casey said as she walked closer towards me.

"Hey…I wouldn't come any closer, I'm pissed off and Leroy hasn't had good action all night, I wouldn't do that if I were you." I said as I pointed the bat

"Are you seriously threatening me with a bat? God, you have changed."

Yea, you know what ..I have changed Casey. It's called being an adult and growing up. I should have never let you stay here. You've been nothing but, a headache since you got here, from smoking pot in my living room before my party which; my coworkers were supposed to attend, to you being a complete inconsiderate slob and Oh, not to mention threesomes in my living room without even asking me if you could have company. It's like you don't care…you know what, I'm over it. I can't take it anymore. You have got to go. I love you but, you clearly don't respect me or my home so, you can't stay here anymore."

Speechless, Casey sat back on the couch and sighed

"Oh no, that "Get out" I said a few minutes ago was for you as well…Like Now.. get your stuff Casey, you've got to go." I said in sadness that I had to even resort to treat my friend this way.

"What? It's like 4 in the morning, where am I gonna go at this hour? She asked

"To Jay's... Maybe you guys can finish what you've started. I don't care at this point" I said

"So, this is how you are going to treat your friend of more than a decade? You're going to just throw me out in the street danm near 5 am in the cold? Come on Alicia let's just sleep it off tonight and we'll talk in the morning."

I walked over to the closet and grabbed her things out and gently placed them by the door.

"Yea Casey, you are my friend of more than a decade but, this isn't how friends are supposed to be...you've got to go..all of you...Out NOW"

As I held the door open Jay and the young woman stumbled out agitated and drunk. Casey fully dressed with her canvases in hand walked through the door and said

"Call me in the morning so we can talk..You're clearly not thinking straight and I know you're pissed at me right now but, we should definitely talk this out."

"I am thinking clearly..You on the other hand have not for the past 5 years.. Look, I wish you the best with your shoots here and selling your art but, I can't help you at   my expense. You've seriously got to get yourself together Casey…but, not while you're in my home..Good night!" I said as I closed the door I should have never opened.

It's funny, now looking back a year later, I should have trusted myself. I knew letting her just pop up here wasn't a good idea but I didn't listen to my gut saying "Nope, Holiday Inn". I wasn't true to myself and I didn't set boundaries in my friendship or establish how I wanted and needed to be treated and because of that the friendship went south. I still haven't heard from Casey, and I'm not even sure if I ever will. I hope she learned something from me … I know I did.

Time in Her Shoes

EARLIER TODAY WHILE RUSHING to catch the train on 13th Street, it seemed everything was on a mission to slow me down. I absolutely had to get to work early this morning to finish editing my article and help my cubby buddy by proof-reading one of her pieces. She had covered for me last Friday as I skipped out the office early to go to a much needed happy hour date with a couple of Mojitos. It was a very hectic week and the college girl inside me who stuck around after graduation was dying to get out and let loose.

The subway was super packed as usual and two cars almost hit me as I crossed Pine Street. I finally made it to the next train, collected myself and caught my breath. The jelly donut, I got up a half an hour early to get, slipped out of my hand and fell right onto my brand new suede Gucci boots…which I had taken two extra writing jobs just to afford, and won a "tug of war" with a woman at Macy's who thought she was going to get the last pair. As I began frantically searching for a tissue to try and save my poor stained boots, I looked up to a white crumpled up napkin waving in my face. It was attached to an old wrinkled hand belonging to an elderly woman who was smiling at me. She was wearing a long dark brown coat with old faux fur that had seen one too many days and had its fair share of stains. Her hair was matted and partially covered by a crochet hat that hid all but a few grays hanging off to the side. She had the most pleasant smile and her eyes glowed like she was 21.

She waved the white napkin at me and said, "Here Darlin', this will help you and those pretty boots."

Then she paused, turned around and said, "Hold on let me grab you another off my dresser."

She then walked to a broken down cart a few feet from us and began searching through clutter packed in it. Immediately my heart dropped. As she looked through the cart, I began thinking less of my early morning catastrophe and more about the poor homeless woman in front of me. She turned around with a McDonald's bag full of napkins and gave me one. I humbly grabbed it ignoring my usual germaphobe instincts. She then pulled out a few more napkins and started wiping down her shoes, which were so worn down structure no longer existed and the right one had a "peek-a-boo" hole in it for her big toe.

"I usually keep napkins for when it rains and the mud gets on them. See, I love my shoes too," she said, "so I know how you feel Darlin…"

Here, I was worried about ruining one of the many pairs of shoes from my closet of endless footwear and this old lady barely had one pair which she greatly appreciated, lived out of a shopping cart, and was just as happy and content about it all.

"I saw you way back over there running and fumbling…just rushing life…rushing, rushing! All the young people now are in such a rush. Let life come on its own. It's gonna' happen whether you're there or not. That's how you messed up those pretty boots. Your mind was running but your shoes were walking. Appreciate your time."

I smiled at her thankfully for the wisdom she was kind enough to share. She didn't have much, yet offered me great advice and the little she had in the form of a napkin. She even tried to help wipe my boots. I then pleaded with her to stop and wiped them myself in fear that she would finish the job. Then she quickly grabbed and wrapped up the jelly donut I dropped on the ground earlier in fear that someone else would take it.

Immediately the life lesson she was sharing with me exceeded the ones coming from her mouth. Her existence at this point taught it all. I stood up and walked to what she called her bedroom and asked her to join me for breakfast at the coffee house up the street. I couldn't stand there and let this sweet elderly woman eat my dirty jelly donut for breakfast. Besides, it was the least I could do for someone who cared enough to give me, a total stranger a piece of what little she owned. Sure, I did think about stumbling into the office late and the homicidal face my cubby buddy was going to give me once her article was ripped to shreds by our editor but I have a funny feeling the day had a totally different lesson in place for me to learn in that moment.

The old woman had two bagels, a piece of fruit along with some fresh coffee and I was glad to be her company.

Smacked by Reality

IF BIRD POOP HAD ANOTHER name, I swear it would be called, "My efforts this past year." Today I came across a lady on the train that looked around 22 years old, not too tall, gorgeous brown skin, and a fashion sense that can be appreciated by artistic gurus in the Philadelphia area. She wore a black pin-striped blazer and a pencil skirt that was work chic and a stunning golden color that screamed: "I'm fierce and I'm here." Her stance was that of a model, perfect posture and she had on a pair of Marc Jacobs black glasses. We started a conversation about the reeking smell of pee and body odor on the train, poking fun at the environmental services that were responsible for clean-up. She seemed very educated and had a down to earth street edge which let me know she was from the area. As our conversation seemed like it was coming to an end she handed me her business card and said "You seem really cool, we should grab a drink sometime"

I immediately agreed and smiled. She seemed cunning in her jokes and very mature, to say the least so, I asked her what she did for a living, she replied that she's a junior partner at a local law firm. With my eyebrows slightly raised, trying not to show how impressed I was by her achievements. I then asked her age and she sighed and replied 27. I couldn't hold in the emotion anymore and dropped my mouth.

"Wow that's impressive, you must be very driven," I said. She then stood up straight, pulled her neat bangs back with her left index finger and said, "No...It's just simple; I wanted something so I went for it. You have to work hard for anything you expect to get even if it means sacrificing potential fun moments. Nothing in life is handed to you. I stood up night after night studying hard in law school while all my friends were partying, getting drunk, and busy indulging in social climbing."

As she spoke, I thought "me, me, and me!' How many umpteenth times I passed out the night before drunk in someone else's dorm room and managed to make it to Literature II second semester at 8 a.m. in the morning was beyond me. I thought of each and every time the sun beat me home before an exam I knew I had to ace. All of these moments flashed before my eyes. How I made it out of college with a 3.8 G.P.A is beyond me and here was this woman years younger than me that was excelling in her career and in life all while maintaining an impeccable fashion sense, confidence, and flawless skin .Yes, I noticed the Gucci pumps she had on her feet; don't judge me…I'm a sucker for fashion.

As the train announced the 8th and Market stop I managed to come back to the conversation long enough to hear her ask me what I do for a living? I then replied, "I'm a freelance writer but, after hearing your impressive occupation and climb to success I have a funny feeling I have a lot of work to do."

All this time, I was so impressed with the fact that I became a writer and contentment had set in. Now that I had reached my goal what is the next step? My friends praise me every time they see my name above an article in the paper or a magazine; which is fine and I'm very grateful but to just settle for "Freelance Writer/Author" isn't enough to say I've made it.

We then both began to get off the train. She went left and I went right and I couldn't help but stop and glance back at how we parted ways. It seemed symbolic, I was walking off to be stagnant and she was strutting off to climb a ladder of success. As I turned around to walk in my direction I smacked into a man with paint all over his clothes rushing to the train carrying a mini ladder. As he apologized and helped me off the ground I saw the ladder and thought to myself. There's my ladder literally. I smiled and got off the ground thinking, How ironic, I found my ladder of success. It was in me and I just needed a little dose of "Wake up" to make its presence known. I now have the ladder...all I have to do is climb it...on to the next endeavor.

Former Snow Flakes

T HERE'S NOTHING LIKE the first snow flake falling over the city. The air is stiff and cold, everyone bundles up in their favorite scarf or hat and it's the middle of "cuffing season" a.k.a. the season to have someone else to snuggle up with in order to keep warm due to the cold weather outside. It only happens once a year, ends the minute the winter season breaks and it's highly beneficial to its participants if conducted the right way. In short, you're guaranteed a great deal.

I sat in my bay window sill, curled up in my bathrobe watching everyone walk by while eating s'mores and double-chocolate hot chocolate which I'm sure my trainer at the gym would probably kill me for. As I admired the clean crisp look of the snow in the city, the phone rang. I was hesitant to picking it up because I normally don't answer the phone before 9 a.m. on a Sunday but, all the caffeine from the chocolate had me giddy so I grabbed the phone. It was a friend of mine who ran into my old High School sweetheart Darryl yesterday while doing some Christmas shopping downtown. She began telling me how great he looked and she noticed there was no ring on his finger. She went on about how much he spoke of me with what she called "A glow in his eyes."

Finally, she quickly snuck in that he gave her his number for me to get in contact with him soon because his flight would be leaving today in the evening around 7:45 and he wanted to see me. I stumbled over not only the phone cord but slipped on two of my shoes all while managing not to drop the phone, in fear I would miss a digit. As I took down the number on a post-it, I kind of felt like a sell out because I was supposed to hate him for the rest of my life, make T-shirts, and advertise on a local billboard in homage to how big of a jerk he was . Allow me to enlighten you, Darryl proposed spring of senior year in high school and dumping me two weeks after graduation; which I was completely oblivious to until he never picked up the phone again. I hung up and resumed to my cozy fetal position by the window sill, except this time my hands were itching and anxious, anxious to dial his number. I stared at the post-it thinking I have two choices, I could be an adult, let go of my fears and meet with him or don't and act as if it never happened.

"What the hell, you only live once," I thought. I jumped up, got dressed, and grabbed my coat. As I headed for the door the phone rang again. "Later," I said to myself, thinking whoever was on the other end of the phone could wait. I waited long enough for this opportunity to present itself again and I wasn't going to wait another minute. The phone continued to ring. I braced myself for the snow, jumped into a cab and headed to my favorite little boutique to grab an outfit that hugged me in all the right places and that doesn't scream, "You need to go to the gym." Luckily they were open and my favorite customer rep Natasha was working. She was very fashion forward and always gave the best advice. I clearly took this as a sign that I had made the right decision to meet up with Darryl again.

After grabbing an amazing outfit plus shoes that would probably make my feet hurt like hell, I quickly hailed the nearest cab. When I got home I had several messages blinking on my answering machine. I assumed it was Jasmine again with some late information about Darryl, so I pressed play and it was the deepest voice I had heard on my answering machine in a while...it was Darryl. Instantly I smacked myself in the forehead because I was so excited and in a rush preparing to meet up with him that I forgot to call and confirm the date. He sighed on my answering machine and said, "Hello, Alicia how are you? I'm not sure if Jasmine talked to you yesterday about having lunch with me today. Unfortunately, that's not going to happen; I have to catch an early flight back home due to my wife being sick. It would have really been nice to see your smile and again I'm sorry. Hope all is well with you and take care."

As my mouth dropped to the floor along with my heart in disappointment I looked over at his number on my bed and I wasn't sure if the frustration came from not being able to see him or the fact that I had actually let him into where I swore to never allow him again. "I see he is still quite the magician", I said to myself. Once again he has managed to not only do an amazing disappearing act but also make a woman appear out of thin air in the form of his wife. At least this time he had the decency to call first. I balled up the number, made sure it made it to the trash this time and resumed to where I should have never left, a place that was familiar, and safe..the world I knew. As I gazed out the window I thought, some things from the past are just better off in the past.

When the trash men came, in the morning outside my window, to collect, I was relieved.

Past Polaroid's and a Heavy Heart

THE CLOCK STRUCK 2 PM at my miniature desk at home and I was still staring at a blank screen. I'd left the office this morning in hopes I would get inspired to write something for Sundays deadline which only was 2 days away, talk about an epic fail. Luckily, I was supposed to go visit my mother's side of the family across the bridge which always left me with a plethora of material. As I abandoned my article to pack for Jersey, I grabbed one of my old journals for my little cousin who is an aspiring poet and surprisingly enjoys my work. As I tucked it in the bag an old crumpled up picture slipped out. I couldn't help but laugh uncontrollably once I recognized the picture. It was an old Polaroid of me and Tremaine hours after prom senior year. And on the front at the bottom, he wrote: "Tell me the truth."

It was an epic night I would always remember. It was our first experience with alcohol and we were horribly intoxicated off of three beers and you could tell by the drunken smiles on our faces. Tremaine was hugging me while wearing a pair of my panties on his head as a result of losing a bet we had earlier in the school year. See, it all started because Tremaine was sure his high school sweetheart Amanda Ragin would lose her virginity to him on prom night. Personally, I knew It wouldn't happen because Amanda was practically a saint in school and the girl lived in church. So after prom, he showed up to Dereck Breecher's Pool party upset with a six pack which he had to give Dereck one for entrance into the party, two and a half for me and my victory and two and a half for him and his loss. I kinda felt sorry for him he had been working on Amanda all school year and was truly looking forward to winning. But, me being the good friend that I am I couldn't just watch him wallow in defeat so in an effort to cheer him up I offered the only pair of panties he would obtain that night…mine. I reached under my poufy dress with way too much beading, shimmied off my underwear and slapped them on his head. We both burst out into laughter and luckily one of our classmates captured another one of our epic moments.

Tremaine was quite familiar with the ladies, tall, good looking and was loyal to his friends. We'd become best friends sophomore year, I could depend on him and tell him anything as long as it was the truth. He had a thing for people being honest with him. He'd always give the best sarcastic advice, was wise beyond his years, and was highly independent due to his mother passing at a young age. We also had all sorts of crazy situations that made our friendship priceless. Either way, I knew I couldn't visit Jersey without seeing him and catching up on old times. I owed it to every epic moment we created in the past. A small part of me was dying to relive those crazy moments again.

After reaching Jersey and spending hours stuffing myself full of Grandma's southern cooking, I was still waiting for Tremaine to return my call. I'd left him several messages already. He reached out to me a little over a year ago but due to my busy schedule, I never got a chance to call him back. Okay, I know what you're thinking, way ahead of you. I should be honest with myself. So, I didn't return his phone calls because we were in two different places in life and the last time we hung out three years ago things seemed pretty awkward. For starters, it was a stretch to get him to come hang out which was unusual for him because he was always the life of the party. But this time he seemed very distant, detached it was if his mind was somewhere else and he drank so much I had to see him home. We didn't hang out after that because things really took off for me career wise. I became crazy busy. I started working at the Inquirer, moved into my dream apartment in Rittenhouse Square and my new day-to-day obligations mixed in was a huge concoction full of busy.

That Saturday morning, I awoke to a text message from Tremaine saying:

"Call in a sec."

So, I went on with my day, helped my dad in his garden, listened to a few of his fishing stories and laughed at every joke which; he tells over and over again as if he never told them before. I went to lunch with my mom and drank one too many Mimosas as a result of hearing her concerns of my love life being replaced by Morpheus, my cat. I also had to hear about my non-submissive qualities, which according to her, are requirements to obtain a man And lastly, her consistent dislike for my bangs, which I tried to explain to her was very fashion forward nowadays.

After lunch, I passed out on my child-like bed and it hit me that Tremaine still hadn't called. Was he brushing me off? How dare he brush me off. He probably has no time because he's in some high maintenance relationship with some pretty stick figure who picks out all his shirts and bed linens in exchange for her affections. He's always had a soft spot for dainty, gorgeous women who have been given their way all their lives by daddy.

"This will end now…he will answer my call, screw that!" I said to myself.

We always promised to at least stay in touch regardless of where life took us and I know I hadn't always picked up the phone but two days in a row of calling? Come on that's a bit mean. Granted I slacked on my end of the bargain but I was willing to put my pride aside and accept the ridicule in trade of catching up with my friend. So I dialed his number again with my fingers crossed…and a female picked up.

"Ummm. I'm sorry I must have the wrong number." As I was getting ready to hang up she shouted, "No, No, are you calling for Tremaine?"

"Yes," I said confused. She then sighed and said, "I'm sorry Tremaine passed away three months ago "

"What?…ummm…he texted me a few hours ago, that's impossible"

"I texted you and told you I would call in a second because I heard your voice message to him. I'm his cousin, Larissa. I currently have his phone now and have been using it since he passed. I needed a phone and his dad, my uncle let me have it and I kept his phone plan. I remember you from high school. Your mom used to make the best banana nut muffins…anyway, I'm sure you don't want to talk about your mom's muffins while hearing your friend just died. So, I'm sorry you had to find out like this…he's in a better place."

"How did this happen?" I asked her.

"He swallowed a full bottle of pain pills. It shocked me too. I would have never thought he would have killed himself. It was probably that bitch Bianca, his X…he didn't take the break-up well."

I slowly dropped the phone in shock and grief. My friend a.k.a. "The Life of the Party" killed himself? I cried and soaked my old childhood pillow. After peeling myself off the bed several hours later, I called his cousin back and got burial information of his grave site. I came to Jersey with plans to see him and dead or alive it must happen.

During the long agonizing ride to the cemetery the next day all the fun memories swarmed around my head. Bonfires, the beach, New Year's Eve parties in Atlantic City, the plethora of women he would beg me to kick out of his dorm room. It was as if I had relived every moment, the horrible taste of warm coronas he would keep in the trunk of his Honda civic was still in my mouth. That same Honda got us all the way to Vegas and back sophomore year right after finals. We were quite the team at one point. Then everything changed. I changed and I knew deep down in my heart I was the cause of our diminished friendship. As the cab driver pulled up to the burial plot I couldn't   bring myself to get out the car. Was this how I was meant to remember Tremaine? Was this supposed to be our last moment? As I looked down at the old Polaroid of us in my hands a peace came over me I then discovered I didn't want this burial site to be the last memory of me and my friend, I owed more to us, more to our kick-ass moments than me sobbing over his plot. This was not the memory I wanted to create. I had the best memories in my heart and right here in my hand.

"Never mind driver, please take me back...back to where I shouldn't have left in the first place."

Be Careful, You May Need Them One Day

I WAS SITTING AT MY DESK twiddling my fingers enjoying the view of Center City, waiting for 5 o'clock so I could enjoy a long island or maybe a Sex On The Beach. As I began to daydream and taste the drink on my tongue I was awaken from my distraction. Clara, My bosses assistant slammed a pile of papers on my desk so hard it spilled my warm latte onto my pink cocktail dress, that fit perfectly snug and which I precisely wore just for happy hour this evening. I frantically began searching for a Kleenex to try and keep the latte from staining. Demanding my attention, she stood there clearing her throat."

"No, no, no Clara, it's okay I got it. Don't worry about it. It's just a $250.00 chiffon-Misty Kitten- limited edition dress tailored to fit. I'm sure I can find it on-line or something. How can I help you?" I said sarcastically as I rolled my eyes.

"Charmed," she said with a straight face as if emotion was a stretch for her. "Morghanna needs you to cover this story this evening. Your point of contact, time and location is in the lengthy email I sent you five minutes ago.

"Whoa, Whoa, today isn't my late day. Fridays are NEVER my late day." I said in hopes her face would crack into million pieces and she would poof into a bat and fly into the farthest cave in fear of daylight. "Give it to McCallister, he's not doing anything," I said as I pointed to him slumped over sleep in his cubicle with a glob of nacho cheese in the corner of his mouth. "He's been sleep since lunch, and plus it's his late day."

"No, your schedule was temporarily revised per the email I sent you, two minutes before I sent you the assignment. Plus Morghanna specifically asked for you to do it." She then continued to sarcastically say, "For some apparent reason she thinks your insight of this story is important due to your art history background. Personally, I have to disagree with her on this one judging by that hideous piece of art you're disguising as a dress. Word of advice don't ever wear that again. Oh and, for god's sakes don't be late. The last time you covered a story in South Philly I had to spend my whole lunch break   listening to

Morghanna rant and rave about you because it almost cost us the story. I'd like to actually eat tomorrow, so be there on time."

"You're talking about the time she threw a cover story on my desk at a quarter to six on a Monday last minute? I was nearly robbed on my way to the subway by some jerk posing as a homeless man begging for change, then groped to death on the crowded train and broke one of my heels trying to chase a taxi who decided to keep a $ 50.00 tip that was supposed to be my lunch money for the week. Yet and still I was able to get the story in by Tuesday morning before Noon." I said as the veins were popping out of my neck."

"Oh stop your whining. Do you think Fredrick Douglass complained when he marched on Washington for equality? Do you think our forefathers whined when they built this country from the ground up?"

I paused in awe that she'd gone to a higher level of ignorance than what she had already attained. "You're not even a citizen, and for the record its Martin Luther King. Please don't ever say that to an African American. It's highly offensive." I said as a squinted my eyes in amazement of how she managed to put pants on this morning without confusing herself.

"That's beside the point…now you have a decision to make. It's either happy hour or your job Albert Einstein.

And I know who he is." She said before walking away while brushing her bangs and leaving traces of that horrible perfume. You know, the overpriced perfume that smells horrible but people buy it just because of whose name is on the label.

As you can see Clara and I did not get along. She started working here about two years ago after Brenda an older lady who made the best brownies on the east coast, got fired.

I couldn't understand it. If there was anyone to fire, it should be McCallister. He always steals supplies for his "Puppy Lovers" support group, or even Ava who takes extra-long lunches and comes in drunk. Hell, fire anyone else but Brenda; don't fire the brownie lady.

It killed the morale around the office; when she left a little piece of my sanity went with her. I literally had nothing to look forward to on "Brownie Wednesdays" anymore. Clara got hired very shortly after Brenda left. She wears high-end couture clothing, has blonde hair with not a split end, Pounds on way too much makeup and walks around the office sticking her nose up at everyone. She has no credentials and never has a kind thing to say. For example; she always says "Word of Advice" and then follows it up with something highly insulting which wasn't really advice at all. It was just meant to sting like a son-of-a-gun." Oh, and might I add, only got this job because she's dating my bosses grandson.

A couple of hours later after finishing up my interview I, Danielle and Cody decided to meet up on 4th and Chestnut for a drink. I couldn't make happy hour but the night was still young. After several Mojitos and a few appetizers later, which I definitely shouldn't have had, we all decided to head to a cigar bar on the 15th Street that Ian just couldn't shut up about. While there, I managed to get two numbers with dates attached to them so I was feeling lucky. As we were walking out of the bar I heard someone grunt and scream down the short block. There were people crowding around with their cell phones out looking at whatever was going on. As we walked closer it looked like there was a drunken man in a fight. I had plans on passing the brawl till I noticed it sounded like a woman. I could see some stilettos that looked familiar through the crowd. As I peeled through the crowd I couldn't believe my eyes, it was Clara from work.

Instantly I pushed through the gentleman in front of me and tried to push the drunken guy off of her. "Hey Jerk, let her go" I shouted. As I entered the tussle Cody and Ian grabbed the gentleman and pulled him away. He quickly calmed down in his dapper fitted tailored suit.

His shirt was all mangled and he'd managed to rip his pants in the midst of the brawl. He was so drunk he was stumbling away and shouting obscenities to Clara. As he left so did the small crowd. I then began to help her up. "Oh my God, are you Okay?' I asked her in surprise that this was even happening. "Who was that guy? Do you know him? Do you want me to call the police?" And as Clara staggered up with my help she said, with a bloody lip, "No, NO! It's alright I know him..."

"Who is he?" I said as I helped her to sit on the curb.

"He's an ass," She said while smearing her makeup. "He's my boyfriend. He's Morghanna's grandson. We have these fights every now and then; it's no big deal, nothing a little makeup can't fix."

"It's not alright, look at your face. Clara, that guy needs to be in the back of a police car, not staggering off into the street to go hurt someone else."

'So what would you have me do? Where will I go? I need him to survive. He takes care of me and makes sure I'm okay financially. When I came to the states I had nothing," She then began trying to stand up

"Hey no, you need to sit down for a minute." I told her. She mustered up strength out of nowhere and stood up and said "No, No there's not going to be any cops. I just want to go. Thank you for your help But, I'm okay."

"Wait. Where are you going?" I asked her. "Do you want me to get you a cab to get home?"

"I can't go home right now," She then took a long pause as she leans against the cold building. "The ass is home. I'm gonna to go to a hotel tonight and this will be all over in the morning. Go home I'll be fine…really." She then began walking up the street and discovered someone stole her pocketbook while she was in the altercation with "the ass."

"Damn it! My pocketbook someone must have picked it up," she let out a big sigh and slumped onto the wall and adjusted her overpriced pumps.

I felt so sorry for her, she was broken. I'd never seen her this low before and I knew I had to do something to help. I offered her my phone. "Is there someone you need to call? Do you have family you can call?"

She turned her head and said, "No, I don't have much family here in the states. It's alright, go home Alicia. I'll be fine thank you for all your help. Really, just go!"

As I took her advice and walked a few feet up the street I saw Clara's Red MAC lipstick on the curb. The same lipstick she wore so much you would have thought it was going out of style. The same lipstick I had grown to hate and envy at the same time. It was on its way down the drain and hanging on for dear life. Now, I could walk away and allow this very expensive beautiful lipstick to go down the drain, or I could pick it up and save it since it was sealed tightly and wasn't broken…damaged a little but not broken. If I save it, it may have further use. I then grabbed up the lipstick quickly and walked back to Clara and stood in front of her. I pointed the lipstick at her and said, "Just because something has fallen to the ground, became dirty or, seems useless doesn't mean it's not worth saving." I grabbed her hand and put the lipstick in it. "Don't lose yourself…don't let yourself go. You are here in the States for a reason and it's not to be someone's slave or punching bag. So what the guy takes care of you. It doesn't give him the right to abuse you. Look, I know you may not be done with him tonight but if you ever want to leave I'm here. If I can help in any way I can let me know. And you don't have to worry about this getting back to the office your secret is safe with me."

She looked up at me and smiled and said "Thanks, Alicia."

"And if you'd like to crash at my place tonight you're more than welcome. It may not be a suite at the Ritz but my home is yours tonight if you'd like. I have a great Cindy Crawford Sleeper you can crash on and an espresso machine that smells like fresh coffee in France minus the noise of course. I quickly grabbed the cab that was coming down the street and we were at my place in no time. I set up the sleeper for Clara and as I was getting ready to shut the light off and head to bed, Clara said, "Alicia, word of advice…"

I smirked in delight that she was back to her old self. "Sure...what?"

"Be careful how you treat people, you never know, you may need them one day."

"True indeed…good night," I said as I smiled and went to bed.

Tall Vietnamese Dream

I WAS SITTING IN A TINY NAIL SALON for about 45 minutes flipping through the second   pile of magazines waiting for the seemingly happy lady of Asian descent to signal me to come to a table. Then all the way at the bottom of the pile it appeared…People Magazine! It had become my thing since the beginning of the Kardashian era. I have piles of them in my closet and stalk the mail man when my subscription doesn't come on time. I occasionally like to catch up on the new face renovations of Kim, ridiculous baby names, and the latest project Kris was managing that would uphold her title of "Pimp Mother of the Year." I found it to be quite entertaining since I had absolutely nothing going on in my social life. Sad to say but, these over-the-top celebrities had become my new social circle. I knew practically all of their names, pets, children, and who had the most recent wardrobe malfunction. I could even predict every extramarital affair that would later be on the books. I probably could catch it on television but, it's nothing like a good juicy read.

While reading an article on Prince Henry's most recent scandal the tiny door chime quickly snatched my attention and in walked a tall Vietnamese man about middle age with clothes that looked a bit small as if he'd outgrown them. It was the same man I noticed picking up trash outside before I came in he was kind outside and even offered to throw away my Wawa cup in the trash can. He came in and instantly started picking up trash inside, emptied all the bins, and swept up the debris. After washing his hands he offered beverages to everyone who waited.

"They must be paying him as extra help so he can earn cash to make ends meet," I thought to myself. This gentleman seemed to be the hardest worker there and I had made up my mind that he would get at least 4 of my usual $10 tip I set aside for the nail technician. Maybe about 15 minutes later he came over and offered me to a table. I was shocked to see he began preparing my nails for a manicure.

"How are you today? Good, I hope. Will you be receiving a manicure?" he asked me.

"Yes," I said shocked that he would be my technician. "I've never seen you here before, are you new?" I asked him.

"You can say that, I used to work for a mortgage company for many years then I came here.'

"Oh really," I said in disbelief. "What did you do?"

"I was a Mortgage Lending Director…very boring job. You sit in an office all day, four walls, and no fun," He then began laughing.

I laughed with him assuming he was telling a joke.

"That was a good one," I said while giggling. Then two of the nail technicians distracted him by speaking loudly in their native language.

"English Please!" he said in a stern voice. "You offend the customers when you do that."

The two women apologized and began speaking in English to one another.

"My apologies miss," he turned back to me and smiled. "So what do you do?" He asked me. I was so shocked at what I just saw that I couldn't respond. This man who was picking up trash, not only was he doing a damn good job on my nails but, he also fixed my only pet peeve about coming to the nail salon, which is when the technicians speak in their native language while pointing at your feet and laughing.

"Umm…I write for the Inquirer."

"Really?" he smiled in amazement. "Is that what you dreamed? Seems like a dream job."

"No," I said I did an internship after college which kinda led to this job and I just stuck with it. Can't complain it…pays the bills."

"Well, what is your dream? What would you do for a living that brings you joy…soooo much joy that you would do it for free?"

"Well, I've always wanted to write my own book, and sell big, like Oprah's Book Club big. Then publish other books, possibly start my own publishing company. Instead, I am writing someone else's dream. You know, sometimes I want to go in my bosses office flip her the bird and tell her I quit. I mean some of the stories they send me to cover are just ridiculous. Do you know I have to cover at least 5 stories just for one to be approved to hit the paper? Do you know how frustrating that is? And It's never what I want to write about you know. I want to write about life…real life."

As I went on smiling dwelling in la-la land of my dreams the tall Vietnamese man stopped and just looked at me with the biggest smile on his face. "See there it is," he said. "Do it!" he said. "Do it! Look how you light up when you talk about it, you deserve that happiness. We all do."

I then cut him off and said, "Yeah but I've got bills, student loans I can't risk leaving my job at the Inquirer just to chase after some silly dream I worked hard to get this job."

"But you're not happy there. And where is your faith in yourself? I was once like you. I worked hard in college   like my father wanted, got my degrees just to clock in and out every day like a machine. In a cubicle, no fresh air, no joy of what I wanted in life. I wanted to own my own nail salon. Sounds silly but my mother owned one and that money from the salon put me and my sisters through college and, provided a better life for us. That nail salon was a service to the community. It made people feel good. I wanted that for myself so you know what I did 5 years ago? I started believing in myself, saved up for about a year-and-a-half, quit my job bought a storefront and opened my nail salon. The first was horribly small but now I own three including this one. I wake up feeling great about going to work. I help other people feel good about themselves all while providing quality service to my community. You see, every accomplishment starts with the decision to try. Don't give up on your dreams. You want to be an author? Fine, do it on the side, save up and make it happen so that one day you can walk in that office and flip your boss the bird and yell "I quit". Okay, maybe not flipping the bird part, but you get my point. Don't sell yourself short and don't ever sell yourself for a paycheck. The human spirit doesn't acknowledge monetary gain. That's why some of the wealthiest people are miserable. Go after your happiness."

"Wow, thank you," I said as I reached for my wallet to pay him for the quick manicure.

"No, no, no. No charge," he said. "Put it up for Oprah's next book of the month." He then smiled and winked at me.

Sometimes, Forgiveness!

S O APPARENTLY WHEN YOUR BIRTHDAY is around the corner you must submit to repeatedly answering the question, "What are your plans?" For the whole month, it seemed inevitable to avoid. Everyone from my florist to the mailman asked me over and over about the big day. While it is a symbol that I am thought of, it began to become a bit annoying this year because of the painful reminder that I am no longer young.

Shortly after wiping off the icing Thompson put on my face at work as my co-workers sang happy birthday near my desk I received an email entitled "This weekend". I instantly got excited! I knew It had to be from Jeremy, a.k.a. Gingi, one of my besties I met at a Temple party sophomore year while in college, which also happened to be my birthday. While in line for the bathroom we discovered we shared the same birthday and instantly hit it off so well, we decided to spend our birthdays together every year after and always had the best time. Whether we were checking out a gallery or drinking in an old karaoke bar in Chinatown, Gingi always knew how to start the party. Unfortunately, we rarely got to hang out much unless he was in the Philadelphia area for a hot second. He traveled a lot because he was an international stylist; dressing celebrities, athletes, socialites, and wannabes who could afford him. He had lots of celebrity friends who invited him to all kinds of cool parties on yachts and exclusive clubs and I would always be more than happy to tag along. It was the most excitement I'd have all year. With that in mind, this year was going to be epic like the rest.

As I clicked on the email my heart raced in anticipation of what exciting plans he made for us this year. It read:

Hey, bae, I hate to do this but, it looks like we are going to have rescheduled for next year. Teyana Taylor is having something in Milan and I can't miss it, Semi work stuff so there is no plus one. I hope you understand. I called your cell but you didn't answer.

Love ya… Ciao!

"Ciao!" I said in rage and disbelief as I finished the email, picked up my phone and looked down at the missed call. How could he dismiss me and our tradition so easily for a "thing" Teyana Taylor is having. As I began typing out an enraged reply about how crappy that was of him and how time spent with "true" friends should mean more to him than "fake industry friendships". Then, something told me to hit delete. As a writer, I believe I should never write out of anger for it will never come out right.

After work, I decided to treat myself to a full body massage and facial at my favorite spa; after all, I didn't need him to have a great birthday, even though it still boiled my blood and stung my soul. I decided to carry on without him. I wasn't going to allow that fact that I got ditched by my birthday twin for some celebrity ruin my birthday.

Before the spa, I needed to stop home and change into something a little more comfortable. As I got off the elevator, I noticed a bouquet of my favorite flowers in a gorgeous vase at the front of my door. As I picked them up I noticed a note that said "I'm sorry …Gingi."

Instantly, I got upset all over again and the rage I had earlier while typing the email reply came over me and I couldn't get my keys out quick enough to rush to the trash can and put the weak "I'm sorry" flowers in it. How dare he think flowers would be enough to make up for ditching a potential epic birthday memory that would stand the test of time. After disposing of the flowers It seemed nothing could cheer me up or distract me from being ditched for my birthday and in retrospect, things were going well but my energy just wouldn't allow me to enjoy the fact things were going right or should I say , really well. My Uber was super polite, the host at the spa not only got my name right which she never does but, she also took 30 dollars off my services since it was my birthday weekend, the spa even had naturally-flavored hibiscus mint cucumber water which I love, and the masseuse was awesome with the perfect amount of pressure yet it seemed nothing could make me happy. As I left the tip for my services and headed out the door I was distracted by a Facebook notification and I stopped right in front of the entrance door. It was a memory picture from last year of me and Gingi at a masquerade party at some swanky lounge overlooking Times Square. Not thinking, I slammed on the glass door and swung it open out of anger.

"OOOhhhh," screamed an older short woman on the opposite side of the door who had been hit so hard by the high handle that she fell to the ground holding her nose.

"Grandma," said a younger girl who ran to the ground to aid her.

"Oh my God, I am so sorry," I instantly said as I realized she was hit by the somewhat heavy door I forcefully swung open.

"Are you okay?" I asked her as I ran to her aide.

"Don't touch my grandmom," screamed the little girl at me out of anger.

"I am so sorry it was an accident. I didn't realize you were there."

"It's a glass door," said the little girl sarcastically. "You were too busy on your phone," she stated then turned her attention to her grandmother.

"Grand mom you're bleeding, "said the little girl to her grandmother out of concern.

I instantly reached into my bag and gave her a napkin. "Please, put this on your nose. Did you hit your head when you fell?" I asked the older woman and she shook her head no. "I am fine," said the older woman as she tried to get

up.

"Oww…My hip" she said as she grunted

"You must have fallen on it. Don't move stay there .I'm going to get help," I said as I ran upstairs to the spa. After explaining to the receptionist what happened and begged her to call 911 she said, "It's okay calm down accidents happen, relax. Go outside and wait for the ambulance while I'm on the phone with 911."

I went back outside, and at this point, quite a few people were standing around and judging by the looks everyone was giving me I'm sure the little girl told everyone what happened.

"We were celebrating my grandma's birthday with facials and she ruined everything," said the little girl as she pouted

I then knelt down to the older woman and said, "The receptionist is on the phone with 911. An ambulance is on the way. I feel horrible, I am so sorry and I can pay for your medical expenses."

"It's quite alright," she said as she tapped my hand.

Shortly after, a police officer came and while crying I gave him my statement as the older woman was being put in the ambulance. I felt like a monster. I watched the ambulance pulling off and luckily I overheard an EMT say the woman's name and which hospital the older woman was heading to and I was determined to continue to express my apologies at her bedside. So, I ran to the nearest florist and told them to give me everything. After leaking out almost 200 dollars on flowers I dashed off to the hospital. When I arrived at the emergency room at Thomas Jefferson while holding a huge arrangement of flowers in both hands I was able to find the older woman lying down alone with bandages on her nose.

"Hello," I said regretfully.

"Come have a seat, It's okay the coast is clear my daughter and son-in-law are at the mini-cafe down the hall," she said jokingly.

"Are you okay? I am horribly sorry. I had no idea you were on the other side of the door. I feel so horrible," I said as I sat down the huge bouquet.

"I can tell judging by that huge bouquet. What did you think I was dead are you going to a funeral, my lord?" she said as she chuckled.

"Your granddaughter said it's your birthday. How are you so happy and I ruined your birthday?" I asked her

I've had 76 of them and they've all been awesome. I guess I was due for a horrible one," she said jokingly.

When she noticed I wasn't laughing she then said, "Have a seat."

"Don't be so hard on yourself. Accidents happen. Hell, sometimes really bad things happen to us and we must deal with it and move on. Life goes on, and I could tell by your face you were horribly sorry. You've said sorry a thousand times. You even offered to cover this ridiculous hospital bill which is unnecessary by the way because I have great coverage. Sometimes you must forgive and move on. I have forgiven you," she said as she grabbed my hand.

"And plus, I guess this birthday didn't turn out so bad because I haven't spent time with my daughter in years. She usually drops my grandchild off and all I see is the back of her license plate. Now, she must be here…and I love every minute of it," she said as she smiled.

A few hours later, after the older woman was discharged from the hospital, I finally got back home and plopped on the couch. I noticed I had a text message from Gingi. I was so exhausted and upset from earlier I completely forgot about my early birthday fiasco. He stated again how sorry he was, begged for my forgiveness, stressed how awkward he felt because for once in 10 years we were apart for our birthdays. He also stated He could tell I was upset because he knew me well enough to know I never write when I'm angry. Then I got to thinking, How could I want forgiveness and not extend it?

I spent all afternoon begging for someone's forgiveness for a careless mistake I made and yet I wouldn't forgive my friend for having to work an event which could potentially soar his career, over just hanging out with me. As I looked over to the right I saw the top of the beautiful flowers hanging out of the trash can and felt like crap. I am so tired of feeling like crap "I said to myself. And then the older woman's words hit me and I thought, "Sometimes you must forgive if you truly want to move on." And after the day I had…I wanted to move on.

I got up, grabbed the flowers out of the trashcan and set them on the island in my kitchen. I took a picture of them and texted Gingi back that I forgave him with a picture of the flowers attached.

The Invitation

THE LIGHT CREPT IN ALONG WITH   THE noise of the 42 bus into my apartment window at about 10 am that morning and for some reason my alarm clock didn't get the hint from the first beating at 9:30 that I wasn't ready to wake up to the world yet. I remembered promising my sister we would do lunch around 12 on 19th and JFK boulevard. So, I grabbed my bathrobe quickly, ran downstairs and checked my mail In hopes I'd avoid running into the fat bald guy from upstairs in 3C so I wouldn't   have to suffer through another awkward conversation that ends in some creepy invite to watch his ferrets mate.

I opened my mailbox and there it was "The big thick envelope." The one thing every single woman dreads, the wedding invitation. It was light purple with engraved black doves on it and addressed to a "Miss Alicia Di'Amato," which is code for "Ahh haa loser I've found someone who's willing to roll over to me every day while you clearly have not…allow me to rub it in as you eat cake that's going to add at least 3 pounds to your midsection and make it even harder for you to find what I have." I rolled my eyes flopped back onto my heaven of a bed hoping like "Calgon" it would take me away. I sighed and thought great! So, not only do I have to suffer through the humiliation of being single at yet another wedding but, I have to spend money on a gift for an old frenemy from college who's marrying some hot shot pulling six figures and probably doesn't need my gift anyways. God, I hope when the couples song comes on I don't sprawl into a crying frenzy that ends up with me pigeon toed in my stilettos and holding onto the bar for dear life by the end of the night.

Finally, after 30 minutes of sopping I peeled myself up off the bed and went into the bathroom to brush my teeth as I rinsed my mouth out I caught myself in the mirror and for some reason couldn't stop staring. It seemed my subconscious had INVITED me to evaluate myself. As I stared into the old mirror trimmed in white tile I no longer saw my face. I saw failed relationships accompanied by faces as reminders of "What If's" plus every horrible choice I made in the past with men. Over the years I've put plenty of potentials on the chopping block and never looked back but, now all of a sudden a piece of paper has caused me to feel like an underachiever. This invite, probably made of recycled paper, has me peeking at myself under a microscope. As I brushed the hair out of my face I thought, "I don't feel like it today. Why beat myself up about the past just because there's no one in my present. It's not like I didn't try and there will be someone in the future."

As I let optimism cover uncertainty I began to believe the little angel sitting on my shoulder to the right and less of the opposite on my left. I wiped my face with a hot towel and thought there could be some good that comes out of this wedding. Maybe I could meet someone that doesn't have a receding hairline and fresh out of AA…Oh, the possibilities!

And In Walked Mr. Right

I WAS STANDING IN LINE at my usual coffee spot on 10th street dying to get my hands on a seasonal only, frozen peach cobbler latte; which came with tiny pieces of real peaches swimming in a sea of steamed milk, espresso goodness, with flaky crust crumbles over whipped cream at the top. In other words, to my taste buds, I was in line at the pearly gates.

While slightly drooling as the young attendant made my drink, an arm smelling of Burberry fresh out the shower reaches over and handed the cashier in front of me a 50 dollar bill and, offered to pay for my drink. Quickly I straightened up my nostalgic face so he wouldn't catch sight of the salivation I had going on in the corner of my mouth. I fixed my posture and slightly glanced over to see the face of the well–manicured, strong hand on the other end of the generous 50 dollar bill. Low and behold, He was tall, caramel and handsome. His smile was impeccable   due to good dental hygiene which clearly started at a young age I'm guessing. He was dressed very well, and his biceps bulged out of his neatly tucked, buttoned-up Armani just enough to be noticed. To "the untrained, hadn't had a date in 3 months" eye, he was gorgeous.

As the cashier handed me the latte It suddenly wasn't as appealing anymore, He had surpassed the need for my mid-day fix, and I was all for it.

After saying thank you he said, "A lady should never have to pay...I'm Brian, it's nice to meet you," he then asked if we could sit down and talk for a while. We talked for hours, he told me about his childhood growing up bi-racial in Gladwyne, how he finished top of his class from PENN and has maintained an excellent career as a stockbroker. The last vacation he took in Ocho Rios and his new workout regimen which inspired me to get back into the gym. He had so much to say I didn't get much of a word in edge wise so by the end of the conversation we sealed the deal for our first date and even exchanged a hug that kept his cologne on me for the rest of the day.

After picking up some food for Morpheus, I called Kate on the 1st floor to come up and have some margaritas while I fill her in about the new beau I'd acquired earlier. Kate is interesting. She's a techy, trekky, and harajuku all in one. You could catch her reprogramming a PC all while watching Star Trek re-runs just for fun and with a face full of make-up. She attended Comic Con every year and thought of pop-rocks as genius.

While chatting over a few a few drinks in my apartment. Then, there was a knock at the door. It was Devin, one of Kate's friends whom I'd shared an occasional flirtation with over the past year since we met. He wore glasses, was a techy, and carried one too many pocket chains with oversized button up shirts. He wasn't my type and often distanced himself from others but was always mannerly, kind and had the cutest messy curls for hair. He came by to drop off some new software for a program she'd worked on previously. I offered him a friendly drink with us and he quickly scarfed it down and made an excuse about having to get home to feed his cat. Being mindful of his previous guarded behavior to social interaction, I didn't mind him cutting out on the girl talk.

A few weeks went by and Brian and I went on all sorts of dates several times a week. Picnics, horse and carriage rides through the city, dinner at all the five-star restaurants and exclusive V.I.P to all the local night clubs were my new life. I was becoming addicted to the fast pace while gobbling down shots of espresso just to stay awake. My new norm had become parading around with this gorgeous man I'd recently found whom, very quickly became my new beau. I decided to give him the title once he asked me to go on vacation with him to Tahiti while holding the very same Tiffany bracelet I'd made slight mention of before. One evening while at work, Brian a.k.a. "the beau" called, and invited me to dinner at his parents' house in Lower Merion. At first, I thought it was a bit soon for family reunions but he seemed really excited about introducing me to his folks so, I kindly agreed and told him I'd be ready an hour before. When we got to his parent's estate it was gorgeous, far from my parent's row home in Jersey. They had huge statues lining the driveway, a gardener and a mid -size vineyard to the left of the house. As we pulled up his parents were already standing out front with his little sister Elizabeth and the family dog whom I discovered after cracking a joke on his name to lighten the mood was named after Brian's grandfather. I mean really, who names a dog "Feebus" They introduced themselves after his mother critiqued my dress and rushed us into the dining hall where dinner was waiting.

Rosemary lemon lamb chops with a braised sauce and tiny little potatoes with roasted carrots gave me the worst rumbles in my stomach so I kindly excused myself from the table and speed walked to the bathroom in fear I wouldn't make it. To my surprise while in the bathroom, I received a text from Devin. He asked if he left his lucky lighter at my house when he came over a few weeks ago and went into a whole spiel about how things haven't been right since. I told him I was on an important date, couldn't talk, and that his lighter was in a safe place. He then asked if I needed anything and if I was safe. Just like Devin to be thoughtful I said to myself jokingly and told him if I needed a getaway car I'd call. After shuffling around in the bathroom for at least 15 minutes I finally collected myself and rushed back to the dining hall but the house was so big I literally got lost. I had been gone for quite some time and didn't want to be rude especially since I was the guest of the hour, plus they were serving lemon crème Brulee for dessert with a side of fresh strawberries. My inner foodie couldn't miss out. As I wandered around the halls I began to hear voices which were a few rooms away. As I got closer the voices sounded familiar, it was Brian and his mother. I quietly hustled to the door in hopes I'd hear the scoop on his mother's verdict of me. It was bound to be revealed and I was anxious to hear any little tidbit I could.

"So....what do you think?" Brian said

"She seems 'Okay'. A little on the plump side but..." and before his mother could finish Brian cut her off "See... What did I tell you? I told you, I'm not shallow."

"Okay, okay. She isn't your usual I will give you that. She's short, a little frumpy, and those glasses, my god! But, she does give the impression that there's some brain activity going on upstairs. Unlike the previous Barbie dolls, you've brought home. My goodness, all they ever talked about was reality TV, watching carbs, fashion, and tanning. You couldn't get an educated conversation out of any of them to save your life. It was unbearable. I must admit it is refreshing to see you with someone completely opposite. I'd rather see you with an ugly whale, who can actually read, rather than a gorgeous skinny bimbo who doesn't think."

"Well, it could have been worst. Could have been a man," Brian said as he laughed. "Hey! We agreed that was just a phase. Brian! That was just a phase. Your father would have a heart attack if he knew about that. It's okay to indulge in our pleasures every now and then but, continuing our lineage is what's important.

"So, you're asking my opinion of her, what's yours because it doesn't actually count if you're not into her?" said his mother.

"That doesn't matter, what matters is I brought someone home who you thought I was incapable of bringing."

"So I'm assuming that's a no," she said as she laughed. "Just make sure you let this one down easy, the last one was a nut and your father and I are not paying any more lawyer fees."

I couldn't believe what I was hearing. Have I been a pawn for a man who had something to prove? A bi-sexual man at that? I don't date bisexual men. I go shopping with them, get Mani's and Pedi's with them. Hell some of them are my closest friends…I love them. But, I do not date them, no matter how gorgeous they may be. And wait did she just refer to me as an ugly whale? I may have a few freckles which I do occasionally pass off as beauty marks and glasses but that's very fashion forward nowadays. She has no idea what she's talking about I am a catch! If her son wasn't so busy checking out the pitcher's crotch, he would have caught me.

As I leaned against the hallway wall in agony, I thought, "Just great! I had a mind to turn that corner and give him and his mother whom must be color blind due to the foundation which was two shades too light for her face, a piece of my mind. But what would that really solve? He would still be misleading and deceitful so he wouldn't have to face the truth about himself, and his mother. Well, judging by the scrunchy and over applied makeup from the 80's, I'd say she wouldn't change either. It's probably better to just cut my losses and get out of here. We've only been dating for a few weeks which wasn't that big of a deal. Plus, after what I heard today I don't ever want to see Brian again, let alone be a part of his family.

So, I took my purse from the coat room, tiptoed pass the dog in hopes he wouldn't alert anyone of my swift departure and grabbed one of the crème Brule's off the butler's tray as he walked by and b-lined it for the door. After the evening I just had, there was no way I was leaving without that. Hell, it was the best part of the visit.

After walking and calling an Uber three blocks from Brian's family estate I couldn't wait to kick my heels off in the back seat and ask the driver to floor it to "Nineteen." They had my favorite drink, the "Ruby-tini" which was much needed right now. As I rubbed my feet during the ride I thought about the red flags I should have seen…the expensive gifts, me never being able to get a word in about myself, the overly-perfect skin. I'd never met a man so obsessed with his skin before. Don't get me wrong, I appreciate men with good hygiene but if you exfoliate more than I do, we have a problem. I think I may have jumped the gun and dropped the ball with this one at the same time. All I saw was a gorgeous man who dressed nice, showered me with lavish gifts, smelled phenomenal, and said yes to whatever I wanted. I never looked at the important things to see if he was a good fit for me and because of that I ended up with a "red onion." That's a guy who looks pretty on the outside but when you peel back the layers and discover what's on the inside, they stink and make you cry. Definitely, Mr. Wrong.

While on the expressway Devin texted me again saying "Hey Alicia, something just doesn't feel right are you okay? Is he behaving? I know you said not to bother you but I just want to be sure ..." I told him I was okay but I had to leave the date early and for him to meet me at "Nineteen'. As I sat at the bar I noticed Devin at the door, he had 3 calla lilies in hand and as soon as he saw me his face lit up like a Christmas tree.

As he approached the first thing he said was "I can't wait to hear all about it"...kissed my forehead and hugged me. Instantly I thought, "In walked Mr. Right"!

Chelsea

WHILE IN THE GYM climbing my life away on the elliptical trying to shed off a few   unwanted pounds I received a phone call from one of my old college roommates, Dani. I contemplated not answering because I knew it involved me committing to some "Save the world "project. Dani worked for "Hands Together" which is a company that quote-on-quote "takes care of the world one step at a time." Dani always advocated for the underdog. I should have known she would end up in this line of work. In college, she fasted for 27 days just to prove that the government was poisoning our food. She damn near killed herself for the cause. I doubt her pancreas ever got over it. I wasn't the most supportive at the time considering I always catered to my obsession for cheese steaks and fries in front of her. She never forgave me for it but I do make a small donation around Christmas to her company which clothes hairless and short haired dogs. Thanks to me there are warm hairless dogs somewhere in the world.

While watching the phone go to voicemail I started feeling bad because I could hear her voice in the back of my head selling me a line about how "no action" is, in turn, an action within itself because if I do nothing to solve problems in the world things will get worst. I promised myself I would call her back after I hit the shower hell, mind as well. I haven't volunteered for anything lately. I just hope this time doesn't involve heights, the care of strange animals, or donation of a body part because I will hang the phone up and will not, I repeat, will not feel bad.

A few hours later while giving my bathroom a much-needed cleaning I received a voicemail from Dani again. "Shoot! I forgot to return her call again." I thought to myself while arm's length in comet cleaner and scrubbing bubbles shower spray. I must return it now before she puts me in the dog house and writes me off as a horrible friend. I couldn't let her down again since a couple years ago I agreed to run a marathon with her and instead ditched her at the 1-mile mark for a couple Mojitos at a bar close by.

After finally listening to the voicemails it was exactly what I thought .So, apparently, Dani was able to get funding for a new enrichment program that would affect inner-city girls from the ages of 7-18 and wants me to help in some way. Maybe it will be easy this time, maybe she needs me to write an article on it to bring exposure to her project.

The following day after talking to Dani and verbally signing my life away, I agreed to meet her at the Community Center on Spruce to see what exactly she had in store for me this time. As I walked in the poorly decorated recreation room there was a room full of young girls of all colors, Spanish, African-American, White, Hispanic and one girl I wasn't sure if she was Asian or Islander Pacific. Before I could mingle Dani ran up to me and swept me away out of the room and before I could get a word in edgewise or even say hi, she then started, "Hey!! Oh, my God, it's been so long. How are you? You look great! So, first let me say I appreciate you volunteering. This project has been moving so slow and then BAM! She said as she smacked her hands together in my face. "It just took off. I didn't know what I was going to do if I didn't get someone for Chelsea."

"Chelsea?" I said confused "Who's Chelsea?" And Dani just kept on talking as if she didn't even hear me as usual. Once she gets going you usually have to wait until she runs out of breathe to get a word in.

"Oh my God you are such a life saver," she sighed and stopped.

Dani was very animated, she spoke a thousand words per minute, was always breathing in positive air just to release it to the world, very enthusiastic and full of way too much energy.

"Yeah, Chelsea, She's an interesting one, but don't worry She's a nice girl. She doesn't talk much and we don't have as much information on her as we do the rest of the girls, only the basics but, we sense she may have a lot going on. "So that's why I saved her for you."

Soooo, what are the limitations as far as the interview? What can't I ask her and are her parents here for me to get consent?" I asked

"Wait, what are you talking about?" Dani played coy

The interview…Isn't that why I'm here, to do coverage on your project?"

"No, No, I need you to mentor her," Dani said in a lowered voice

Immediately I got horrid flashbacks of the last child I mentored which didn't go well. I pray he grew back that patch of hair in the middle of his head that a disgruntled monkey got a hold of during a trip to the zoo.

"Shit Dani!...NO!" I yelled as I walked past her in hopes I could slip out the front door which wasn't too far away.

"Hey! Hey! Watch the language, but please, please...Come on Alicia..."

"No! I'm not doing it! I already told you I'm not doing anything that has the hazard of me screwing up someone's life and this has hazard written all over it! Look, I'll do your soup kitchens. I'll donate some money. Heck, I'll even pick up trash in the streets for your little "Clean City project," which by the way gave me poison ivy in hard to reach places. I'll even help with your "Stray Cats Deserve Organics Too" program or....WHATEVER it's called... But I am not doing this."

She then began her spew which usually makes me feel horrible.

"Alicia, you have the opportunity to positively affect a young girl's life here. You don't get opportunities like this every day. Come on now this is a chance to take care of the world, one step at a time."

"Did you just use the company slogan on me. Really?" I said with my eyes squinted in disbelief she'd stooped so low.

She then walked over to me and I could see the sincerity and desperation in her eyes.

"Okay look...I really need you on this. You're the nicest person I know. You're successful, driven, you have a good heart. You have a way of being able to connect with people. I know you'll be a great impact on this girl. She kind of reminds me of you," she said as she smiled.

"Don't do that,"I said as I rolled my eyes.

"Do what?" she asked deceptively.

"You tap into my emotions, and then while I'm emotionally vulnerable you go in for the kill a.k.a. say I remind you of something or someone as if their demise could be me and that's so unfair and very cheesy," I said and then smiled.

"I know that smile, "said Dani pointing at me and walked over and hugged me uncontrollably.

"You're going to do it aren't you? She asked.

"Fine! I'll do it. But is this a tax right off? And no trips to the zoo, right?" I said

"Right...so let me introduce you guys and you can get started," Dani said as she walked me towards Chelsea.

"Whoa, wait don't I need to know something about this kid? Give me some information before I meet her like how old is she? Where is she from? What are her likes and dislikes? Something"

"Well, like I told you, we don't know much about her other than what Children and Family Services shared with us because she doesn't talk much, she just writes or sits quietly to herself. They referred her here because her mother has an open case with them for abuse and   neglect, now whether it was towards Chelsea or her other siblings I'm not sure but either way, she's here."

"Abuse and neglect," I asked sadly. "And that's all you guys know about her?" I asked puzzled

"Well, I mean you can look at her and tell she may be having troubles at home unfortunately by her appearance, she bites her nails a lot which is a common sign of anxiety, always separated from the other girls, and sometimes she stares off and is unresponsive, like she's stuck in a memory or something. And I'm almost sure she has PTSD from god knows what traumatic event. You know what; come to think of it there was one thing the social worker shared with me about her medical history. Apparently, when she was 6 she got in between her parents while they were arguing to try and stop them from fighting and one of the parents accidently hit her but instead caught this huge chain that was hanging with their hand by accident and instead of just smacking Chelsea out the way, they smacked her with the chain as well. The social worker said the brother told her everything," Dani whispered

"Whoa," I said.

"Chelsea flew across the room and was out of it for hours at the hospital," Said Dani

"That's horrible."

"Yeah, these girls are truly special Alicia because with all they've been through a lot at such young ages. They are still here, still moving forward, with all their horrible memories of the past, and all their current harsh living situations at home they are still able to smile … with our help, maybe the'll be able to see a brighter future. That's why we're here and that's why I needed you here as well," Dani said

As Dani kept talking I Instantly I began feeling horrible about my reluctance to help. I couldn't imagine what my life would have been like If didn't have my mom and dad who loved me or worst, abused me. I've truly got to start opening my eyes a bit more. This always happens with me; I get completely wrapped up in my day to day life and think everything is about me. I forget about the world around me and become a bit selfish. Maybe Dani was right, maybe this is an opportunity to help this kid and positively affect her life. A mentor might help and according to the universe, that's me.

"So, in general, she's 11 years old. She's from the North Philadelphia area, has quite a few siblings. Her brothers come to pick her up every night. They seem pretty well mannered but, I can say I can't help but notice they share clothes so I'm sure there is a lack of funds at home."

"Share clothes?" I asked as I looked at the little girl picking at her skin and biting her fingernails in an oversized t-shirt which according to Dani, may belong to one of her brothers.

"And that's all you guys know about her?" I asked puzzled.

"Well, I mean you can look at her and tell."

"Well yeah, I've only seen her in literally 4 different outfits. I've seen the same thing on the brothers as well. They definitely swap clothes. So, Last week I took some petty cash and picked up a few outfits for her and the stepfather brought them back here and was quite angry. I couldn't understand it you would think they'd appreciate the kind gesture and then when I spoke to her mother she was defensive as well and begged me to stay out of her business. So whatever you do for her it has to be something the parents don't pick up on or won't see. Honestly, I think your best bet with her is to talk to her, get her to open up. See things positively and hopefully, that will help her," said Dani as she lead me over to the young girl with glasses in the corner by herself.

"Chelsea, this is Ms. Alicia. She's going to be your mentor for the next couple of months. Come a little closer and say hi…Come on," said Dani as she reached out to hug her.

"Hi I'm Alicia, and you don't have to call me Miss. It makes me sound old," I said as I giggled.

"Can we have a seat over here just the two of us so we can get to know each other better?" I asked her.

Chelsea just shrugged her shoulders and walked back over to the table and I followed.

"So tell me about yourself, Chelsea," I said with a smile hoping she would just open up but she didn't she sat there and said nothing as I grinned stupidly like a Cheshire cat. I was becoming desperate to break the ice especially since I was now fully committed.

"Okaayyy, I'll go first. I'm originally from Philadelphia, like you. I'm a writer for the Inquirer, My favorite color is pink. I have a pet cat named Morpheus, and my favorite music artist is Colbie Calet," I said.

"So, you're like a real writer?" she asked me.

"Yeah, I get assignments to go out and interview people and then I write about it and they print it in the paper."

"Wow, that's so cool," she said as her eyes lit up. I would love to be a writer someday," she said as she pulled out a few pieces of folded up pieces paper with writings on it out of her pocket. She unfolded them, sat them on the table, and slid them over to me.

I picked up the papers and handed them back to her and said, "You already are."

She smiled and fixed the oversized glasses on her face. Then she unfolded one and said, "That's for you, you keep it, it took me two days to write that," she said.

Great, I thought to myself, a breakthrough. We sat and talked for 2 hours almost. I even offered to give her a tour of the Inquirer so she could see how the process works. She told me about school, that she was an A-student, and how the kids picked on her because she didn't have much and wore glasses. All in all, the evening was a success.

Two days later I took a half day from the office in an effort to have enough time to grab Chelsea a journal from this little stationary store on Locust Street so that all her writings could be in one place. The plan was to meet her and bring her back to the office in enough time before everyone went home. To my surprise when I got to the Community Center, Chelsea had left a voice message and stated something came up and she couldn't go. I was disappointed, I had talked her up to a couple of my co-workers and they got on board and agreed to show her some of their work as well.

A whole week had passed and still no Chelsea; Even Dani became concerned because she would usually come every other day since the program started. I was   so disappointed sitting outside of the center with a now cold latte in one hand and Chelsea's new journal in the other but something told me to do more as I sat there thinking and worrying about her. So I ran in and got Chelsea's address from Dani and decided I would take a trip over to her house and check up on her.

As I got off of the Broad Street train at Allegheny I read the address on the paper and went to what I thought was her house but it appeared to be an old tiny garage like building with only one tiny window on the 2nd floor and only a wooden rickety door on the 1st floor. I just knew I had to be lost and then a man walked by and stepped up to a house a few doors down. I knew he just had to know the area enough to help me.

"Excuse me, Sir; can you help me, please?" I said as I walked over to him.

"I'm looking for 21 Rosewood Street," I asked him while holding up my post it with Chelsea's address on it.

"You're standing in front of it," he said as he giggled at me.

"Right here?" I said confused as I pointed at the raggedy building.

"Who are you looking for?" he asked as he walked over to me.

"I'm looking for a girl named Chelsea. She's about 10 or 11 years old, wears glasses. I think she has a few brothers that live with her."

And before I could finish he said, "Yup, they live right there. I doubt if they're home though, her mother's in the hospital. They were fighting again last night."

"Again?" I asked.

"So this must happen often?"

Yea, they fight all the time. The kids are all in the mix too, cops get called, and then everything goes back to normal. They'll be back though I'm sure."

"That's horrible…and the kids see all of this?"

"Yea, them kids all screwed up, left home alone all the time. My sister feeds them on Fridays cause the mother works a lot. Children and Family Services in and out of there frequently. It's a mess.

"Well, would you happen to know where I can find Chelsea?"

"Nope, all I know is the mother is in Jefferson Hospital from what I hear she's not doing too well. She may be there, I'm not sure."

"Oh My goodness! Thank you for the information," I said

"No problem, and hey if you see the older brother up there tell him I'm still waiting on my bike"

"Okay, I will and thanks again for the information," I said as I turned to rush for the train.

I couldn't believe some of the things I was hearing about Chelsea and her family. I can't imagine how terrible it was for a kid to have to witness some of the stuff Chelsea's neighbor was telling me. There was no doubt in my mind she suffered from anxiety, depression and maybe even PTSD.

About an hour and a half later as I walked down the hall of Jefferson Hospital I noticed three children sitting outside of the nurse's station and as I got closer I saw Chelsea laid on an older young man, her brother I assumed.

"Chelsea?" I called out, in relief that I found her after all the day's disappointments.

As she heard me call her name "Alicia?" she said puzzled while getting up and wiping her eyes in amazement. "What are you doing here?" she said

"Can I talk to you? I know this may be a bad time," I asked her.

She immediately got up and we walked down the hall to a few available seats near the emergency room entrance.

I heard what happened to your mother your neighbor told me, I'm so sorry," I said to her as we sat down.

"My neighbor? What he look like?"

115

"Tall guy lives a few doors down from you," I said

"Oh, Mike, he's always in our business."

She looked numb, tired, and exhausted. She had on shoes that were so worn down they barely had soles and her hair was matted to one side. My heart broke watching her in that moment but I knew this poor child didn't need anyone else's emotional baggage so I held back the tears.

She shrugged her shoulders and said "You know, it isn't as bad as it seems. Mom is a good mom. I know Mike probably told you some things about her but, I don't want to be anywhere but with my mom."

"Oh, and I won't be coming back to the center anymore. The social worker is gonna get us into a battered women's shelter this time in upstate Pennsylvania somewhere. Maybe now I'll be able to sleep in peace at night with no mean people. Don't have to worry about nobody touching me anymore, making me do wrong things. Don't have to worry about getting beat for having fun, being a kid…for being me. Maybe there'll be silence. Maybe the sun is out all the time there or maybe there'll be a playground nearby with ice cream trucks and water ice stands. Who knows right? My brother said when they send you to these places they hook the kids up with new sneakers, clothes, and everything. Way better than these,"

She said as she pulled part of the rubber sole off of her sneakers. That sound like heaven to me." Said Chelsea

She looked at me with a sad smile. You know the ones where your lips are forced to smile but your eyes are horribly sad. For some reason I could relate, it connected to a deeper part of me. I felt it. I wanted to be realistic with her but her dream was probably the only thing keeping her sane at the moment. In hopes of making her smile I pulled out the pink polka dot journal, I bought for her.

"I have something for you," I said as I put it in her hands. "Do me a favor, No matter where you go or what happens, don't ever stop writing. I don't care if its two words on a page. This is your book, your story. Don't ever stop telling your stories and writing your poetry."

"It's pretty thank you," She said as she smiled and flipped through the empty pages.

Then she reached into her pocket and said I have something for you. She pulled out another folded piece of paper like she did when we first met grabbed my hands and put the paper in it.

"Open it," she said as she stared at me with a scared urgent look.

As I opened the paper it had two words on it, LET GO I turned to look at her out of complete confusion and she was gone. The Emergency room began fading away right before my eyes and disappeared. There was nothing anymore, no sound, just silence. I was alone.

Damaged Goods

(Phone rings)

"Good morning Doctor Ramirez, Ms. D'Amato is awake," said the attendant.

"She's conscious and talking?" asked the anxious doctor.

"Yes, not much but she understands and is responding," said the attendant.

"I'm on my way."

As the well-dressed, concerned doctor entered the office, there awaited two attendants and his client of many years; A woman who he'd grown attached to due to their long-standing relationship with treatment and therapy.

"Hello everyone," the doctor said as he laid the brown cashmere coat over the back of the office chair.

"Thank you gentleman, I think I have it from here," he said as he excused them from the room.

"Ms. Di Amato, I am Dr. Ramirez I am a spiritual therapist and I'm here to help you. How are you feeling?" He asked her

"Spiritual Therapist. I didn't request a priest? Who are you?" she asked him in confusion.

"I am a spiritual therapist, not like you may think…I went to school many years to become a psychiatrist, I Have many degrees but I say spiritual therapist now not in a religious sense. It more so represents my beliefs and ideals that we are spirits moving through this lifetime and how to cope with the human experience.

"Whatever," she said as the medicine she was given earlier began to wear off.

"So, how are you feeling?" he calmly asked again in hopes she would open up.

"Honestly, I don't know, what am I doing here? How did I get here?" She said confused and irritable

"Why don't you tell me? Why don't we start with what you remember before you awoke here?" he said as he leaned back in the leather chair observant

"I was mentoring this kid and I was in Jefferson Hospital with her and her mother. Her life was so sad." She said as more sadness overcame her and she stared at the floor "I wanted to be there for her and she…" as she stumbled over her words and scrounged up her face in confusion.

"…It was weird. She gave me one of her poems, or so I thought that's what it was. When I unfolded the paper it said "LET GO" on it and then I looked up and she was gone, everything was gone. Then I woke up here to some strange room with hospital staff and people I don't know."

"Why do you think you were there Chelsea?" he asked

"What?...I told you I was there to catch up with her, I wanted to give her a book I purchased for her, and why are you asking me this? And who are you anyway?"

Then before he could answer she frantically said, "Wait. Did you just call me Chelsea? My name is Alicia, Alicia D'Amato. What the hell is going on?" She yelled as she stood up.

"Calm down Ms. D'Amato, you are safe here I assure you…Please have a seat," he said calmly as he pointed to her chair. She then paced the room a little more and then decided to have a seat

"I am your Therapist, Dr. Ramirez and I have been for ten years now," he said as he got up and walked over to her. He pulled out an iPhone and began showing her pictures.

"See, I was there at your high school graduation," he said as he showed her the first picture.

"I was with you when you had that meltdown senior year in college and you thought you wouldn't graduate."

"I took you out to dinner to celebrate when you started working at the Inquirer...you were so happy," he said as he smiled and showed her pictures of the celebratory dinner.

"And I am here now."

She looked up at him in amazement. Slowly, memories began coming back to her. She then put her head down into her hands and said, "Oh my God, what is going on? What is wrong with me?" she sobbed out loud.

"One minute I am on this journey to completing myself and making sense of the things that are missing in my life and the next I am in a ...whatever this place this is, without a clue. What is wrong with me " she said

"It's not about what's wrong with you...It's more about what happened to you. You have experienced a large amount of trauma in your life, Chelsea, Catatonia can occur when someone in your position.." she then cut him off

Why do you keep calling me that ...and where have I heard that name before?" She said as she tried to make sense of her current confusion. she squinted her eyes and looked around the poorly painted office.

"That's it," she shouted as she stood up. "The little girl…the little girl I mentored. Her name was Chelsea…Finally some clarity." She shouted and smiled

"Doctor Ramon or whatever your name is…that was the name of the girl I was talking about. She's probably long gone by now. Her mother and brothers were supposed to be going upstate Pennsylvania or something like that. Damn it! I wanted to help her," She said as she sat down.

"You did," said the doctor. "You did help her, and you are now. As crazy as this sounds, you have made progress. You have finally come face to face with the most troublesome part of your past. The one thing you have been running from all these years. Ms. D'Amato, I think it's time. Please have a seat" he said to her again to brace her for the news she would hear once again

"I want you to hear me clearly…Your name is Chelsea D'Amato, not Alicia D'Amato. Alicia D'Amato was your mother. Your friend Morgan who had a mental breakdown a while ago was you. That little girl you have been so engulfed with…is you. That was you when you were a little girl Chelsea. That moment that you can remember up until, and everything fades away at the hospital was the day your mother passed away and it changed everything for you. Each and every experience you have reflected on was a version or an important moment of your past. You have been through a lot of trauma growing up which causes you to have these episodes of serious anxiety, high stress, amnesia and you become comatose while reliving things in your subconscious. But, this time you have come very far. You've literally been with your inner child. You have an objective point of view about your childhood. What were you feeling?"

As the doctor spit out his analysis for her recollections, small things started coming back to her and it began to make sense like the guy Darryl she remembered vaguely was also her father's name, a man who'd jumped in and out of her life as he pleased and whom she would always welcome with open arms and be disappointed time and time again. The best friend she grew up with who didn't, in turn, commit suicide but, really died from a heart attack in his sleep by worrying about woes that weighed on his heart and in life .and of course the man with the sharp grey patch of hair on the front of his head who while in the beginning of her journey was there in the crowd as her friend was being carried away warned her, "The universe unfolds as it should in all things great and small and everything happens for a reason" was the man sitting in front of her. The man who had been her therapist and support for years.

As the tears began to run down her face in realization "I can't... I can't...I can't..right now." She said as she covered her ears, cupped her head in her hands and began crying profusely

"Ms. D'Amato it's alright stay calm...calm down. Do you want to talk about something else? We don't have to address this today?" He asked her in hopes of keeping her from exploding in rage.

She screamed, "I can't" louder as tears and snot ran down her face and hit the floor. She grabbed the chair and threw it to the poorly painted walls. Two attendants immediately, busted in to assist the doctor. They heard the chaos all the way into the hall and grabbed the other items she was preparing to throw out of her hand and instantly sedated her.

"No, No what are you doing??! I didn't ask you to sedate her..." said the doctor in rage at what they'd just done.

"We don't need your permission if a client is in immediate danger to themselves or others we are to sedate them," said the angry attendant while directly staring the doctor in his eye. "Good thing we had this on call," he said as he held the needle up to the doctor's face.

"She was close to a breakthrough and you had no right to do that, I was fine and she would have calmed down, I know...I've been her therapist for 10 years."

"You don't practice here, we only called you as a courtesy since you know the director and expressed some concern for the girl but we have a job to do." They said as they picked her off the floor and carried her to her to her room.

"Ring, Ring!" went the Doctor's cell phone a week later as he sat at brunch with a few colleagues. He looked down at the cell phone and the number looked familiar but he was a little unsure.

"Excuse me I should take this," he said as he stepped out in front of the tiny corner bistro. "Hello?"

"Doctor Ramirez?" said the delicate yet confident voice.

A deep sigh came from the other end of the phone and nstantly the doctor knew who it was. He was relieved he chose to take the call.

"How are you?" he asked.

"I'm alright Noel."

The doctor smiled in appreciation that she remembered his name; for this was a sign that she was coming to the realization of things.

"How are you feeling?"

"Exhausted…tired…I don't know, I just want it all to go away," she sighed "I want to LET GO. All these memories of the past are too much. I don't want them anymore. I want to be happy. I want to live without being reminded of the mental abuse, the physical abuse, how it felt to not eat, how it felt to have to sleep in cars, to not have underwear as a little girl and my vagina constantly be infected from wearing boys clothing and can't wash them, how it felt to be beaten till my skin changed color," She said as she looked at her arms and rubbed them as if she could still feel the bruises, how it felt to be motherless, to scream out to her and she couldn't hear me, to be asked to do things to him I didn't want to, and be sexually abused over and over and can never tell anyone because no one would believe me, to have no friends…no one who understands, to have to watch my brothers, the only people who understood what I was going through leave me, to grow up alone. I don't want those memories anymore. Sometimes it's just easier to not be her. So you don't have to be reminded of what she's gone through."

"Our past is a reminder of how far we've come. It's an imperative part of our life's blueprint and while yours may be very troublesome and hard to accept, you must try to remember the good ones as well Ms. D'Amato. Listen, I am at an engagement and should be done shortly. I had plans on stopping in and checking up on you this afternoon but I can come sooner if you'd like. I'd love to discuss this further with you. You sound as if you've made progress and that's great...I'm happy for you." said Dr. Ramirez

"It's Okay... you can call me Chelsea. And I'm leaving today so that won't be necessary," she said

"Wait...Today?! Why so soon? You've made such progress...I think if you just..."

She quickly interrupted him, "Doctor, it's time I am honest with myself. This morning I woke up and as hard as it was for me, I looked in the mirror for the first time in weeks and saw me...Chelsea...peeking beyond the chaos. She's there and I must continue to move all the crap aside for her to finally breathe and be happy in her own skin. It was so easier to just not be her so I didn't have to be reminded of what she went through. I have to get out of here and continue to work through things without all the chaos and pacifying... I'm not 18 anymore...If I want to really move past this It has to be my journey and my journey alone. I've got a lot of work to do on myself. But please don't worry. I will be okay." She said

"Well, let's set up a session for later this week we can meet at my new office near 2nd Street and I'll grab some of that tea you like from the Italian market..." he said in hopes he could continue the work he'd already done with her.

"I want to thank you for all you've done over the years. You have been more than a therapist. You've been a confidant...a friend. But, this is where we part ways. I must figure this out on my own."

"Chelsea?! Don't do this... you've come so..."

"My brother is here...I gotta go...Take care!

"Chelsea....Chelsea?!!..Hello?"

As her phone disconnected, Dr. Ramirez stood outside of the quaint bistro in shock staring at the cell phone in his hand, destitute, waiting for the returned call that never came...

About the Author

Christina Collins is from the Philadelphia and Southern New Jersey area. She discovered her love for writing and creating stories at a very young age. She began writing poetry at the tender age of nine as a means of self expression. While in grade school she became known for "writing songs and rhyming words" Christina later discovered she could turn her poetry into songs and her classmates would listen. Eventually she ended up using song format to get others to listen to her poetry. Christina expanded her skills by joining the drama club and started writing school plays, and eventually a movie script called "consequences". Christina attended The College of New

Jersey after high school and Majored in Communications: Radio and Television Production. It was there she learned to create segments and incorporate her first love of writing into scripts. During and after college Christina ventured into the film production world as a Production assistant, camera tech, and later a host and associate producer at a local broadcasting network in South Jersey. Shortly after parting with the network Christina Started working on a novel loosely base on a seemingly well-put together woman who was forced to face her inner child entitled "Saving Chelsea. Christina now resides in Philadelphia working in the public health sector helping to change lives for the better.

To My Supporters

For every person who has sat at any show under my voice, read any of my pieces on line, opened the pages of this book, booked me for any event, shared any of my posts for this book on social media or, greeted me with words of encouragement and kindness, I am humbled and eternally grateful because you've helped shaped the pathway that led to this moment. Without you, this would be a broken chain … I thank you with great humility and appreciation for all the support. God bless!!

www.ingramcontent.com/pod-product-compliance
Lightning Source LLC
Chambersburg PA
CBHW020646250626
47154CB00008B/2833